Harbor Me

ALSO BY JACQUELINE WOODSON

After Tupac and D Foster

Behind You

Beneath a Meth Moon

Between Madison and Palmetto

Brown Girl Dreaming

The Dear One

Feathers

From the Notebooks of Melanin Sun

The House You Pass on the Way

Hush

If You Come Softly

I Hadn't Meant to Tell You This

Last Summer with Maizon

Lena

Locomotion

Maizon at Blue Hill

Miracle's Boys

Peace, Locomotion

Harbor Me

JACQUELINE WOODSON

 Nancy Paulsen Books

Nancy Paulsen Books
an imprint of Penguin Random House LLC
375 Hudson Street
New York, NY 10014

Library of Congress Cataloging-in-Publication Data is available upon request.

Printed in the United States of America.
ISBN 9780399252525
1 3 5 7 9 10 8 6 4 2

Design by Marikka Tamura.
Text set in New Century Schoolbook LT Std.

For Lena and Alana, who harbor so many

And for my family, who harbors me

We'll leave now, so that this moment will remain a perfect memory. . . . Let it be our song, and think of me every time you hear it.

—Betty Smith,

A Tree Grows in Brooklyn

1

We think they took my papi.

It's over now. Or maybe it isn't. Maybe, even as I sit on my bed in the dying light of the late afternoon, it's beginning again. Maybe Ms. Laverne is looking over the new class list, her finger moving down the row of names. *Maybe her,* she is thinking. *And him. And her.* But it won't be the same. It won't ever be the six of us together again.

We think they took my papi.

My uncle is a musician and a storyteller. He says the hardest part of telling a story is finding the beginning. I've pulled the voice recorder from my closet and have it sitting on the middle of my bed now. When I press play, Esteban's voice fills my room. It is scratchy and faraway-sounding, but still, Esteban is here again and all of us are sitting in our small circle in a place we called the ARTT room.

Nobody knows where he's at.

Outside, a blue jay perches on the edge of a branch. Ailanthus tree. Tree of Heaven. Ms. Laverne taught us that. It's the same tree the girl in *A Tree Grows in Brooklyn* saw from her fire escape. The thing about that tree was it could grow anywhere. And keep growing. And that was the *metaphor*: that even when things got really hard for everyone in that story—even when the dad died and the mom had to scrub more and more floors to make money, even when the kids didn't have anything to eat for days and the apartment was freezing—the tree kept growing. The main character, her name was Francie—she was like that tree. Ms. Laverne said that all of us—Esteban, Tiago, Holly, Amari, Ashton and even me—we're like that tree too.

My uncle is moving out tomorrow. He's really the only parent I've ever known. He says, *This is a beginning.* He says, *Now you'll have two houses to go to.* He says, *You're twelve now, Haley. You're ready.*

But I'm not ready.

This afternoon, I miss everything.

I miss my uncle even though he is upstairs packing. I miss the ARTT room, I miss Holly and Amari arguing and Ashton pushing his hair away from his forehead. This afternoon, I miss Tiago's dreams of the sea and Esteban's poems and all the stories we finally trusted each other enough to tell. I miss the beginning of our story together. And the deep middle of it.

Once there were six of us. Once we circled around each other, and listened. Or maybe what matters most is that we were heard.

Downstairs, my father is playing the piano—soft, sad notes floating up from the living room. The piano is old—found on the street a few blocks away the day my father moved back home. My father, uncle and three other men lifted it up the stairs, then had to remove the door to get it inside. It's an upright—scratched wood and yellowing keys. My father took a whole day tuning it, and now the notes move through the house, dipping down at the end like tears. Rising up like prayer. Upstairs, I can hear my uncle moving from dresser to bed and back again and I know he is neatly folding shirts and sweaters into his suitcase. Most of his stuff is already downstairs. Boxes line the hall by the front door. His favorite chair is draped with a blanket. His guitars are stacked in their cases beside it. Tomorrow, he will move to Manhattan and start his new life. *I'll be the bachelor I was always meant to be,* he said. Then, seeing the look on my face I failed at hiding, he added—*And I'll be back every single Sunday to spend time with my most favorite person in the world.*

I don't remember a life without my uncle in it.

In two weeks, I'll begin seventh grade. My best friend, Holly, will be there. But there will be holes where Ashton, Amari, Tiago and Esteban once were.

We think they took my papi.

I play the first words of Esteban's story over and over as my father's song lifts up to my room, as my uncle packs above me, as the blue jay perches in the Ailanthus tree. As the world keeps on spinning.

2

That first week of September, the rain wouldn't stop. Rivers ran down along the curbs, and at the corner near our school, cars had stalled in the middle of the huge pools of rainwater. Even though it was still warm outside, our classroom felt damp and a little bit cold. Some of the kids were playing with those spinner things. One boy, whose name I forget, had his head down on his desk. I remember his dark curls, the way they fell over his arm. For some reason those curls spiraling over his arm and down onto the scratched-up desk made me sadder than anything. There were eight of us then. Our small class had come together because the school wanted to try something new: Could they put eight kids together in a room with one teacher and make something amazing? Eight *special* kids.

Even though they didn't say it, we knew there was something different about us. We had all been in the big classrooms before, and our learning felt like a race we were losing while the other kids sped ahead. We made believe we didn't care that we learned differently, but we knew we did. And the school knew we did. The school knew we got laughed at and teased in the big yard and that some days we faked stomachaches and sore throats to stay home. It was only September, so no one knew if this experiment would work. But our teacher, Ms. Laverne, was tall and soft-spoken and patient. We loved her immediately. And the school itself had huge windows and brightly colored walls. My uncle said it was one of the best schools in the city. I had been there with Holly since first grade, so I didn't really have any other schools to compare it to. But if nice teachers and rooms filled with lots of windows made something "the best," then I guess it was true.

By the end of that rainy week, the boy with the curls had moved away and another girl's mom had come in and fussed about her daughter being smarter than *those children* while Ms. Laverne shushed her and guided her and her daughter gently out of the room. The girl looked like she wanted to sink into the floor and disappear. We never saw her again, but sometimes I wonder what it would have been like if she had gotten a chance to be a part of the ARTT room, if she'd gotten to hear what we heard, see what we saw. After she and the curly-haired boy left, only Ms. Laverne and the six of us remained.

An hour after class started on that Friday, Esteban came in, his head down, his hair slicked wet against his forehead, his Yankees cap dripping with rain. He walked straight to his seat without looking at the rest of us. I watched him sink into his seat so sadly and heavily, it felt like the whole room shivered. His jacket was way too big for him, the shoulders hanging down his arms, the sleeves falling over his hands. I didn't know Esteban yet. I didn't know anyone but Holly, really. But I wanted to go over to him, hug him hard. I didn't care how dripping wet he was. No one should ever have to look that sad.

Do you have a late pass for me, Esteban? Ms. Laverne asked. She was standing at the front of the room, her arm stretched out toward the smart board. I don't remember what was on it, maybe a globe. Our tiny group that year was a fifth/sixth grade class—this too was a school experiment.

Is everything okay? Ms. Laverne's dark brown face was crisscrossed with worry.

Esteban shook his head. *I don't have a pass,* he said, his voice breaking. *We think they took my papi. Nobody knows where he's at.* He put his head down on his desk, his face turned toward the window.

Ms. Laverne went over to Esteban's desk and bent toward him, her hand on his back. They spoke softly to each other. Maybe they spoke for five minutes. Maybe it was an hour, I don't remember. That was a long time ago. So much can change in a minute, an hour, a year.

3

While Ms. Laverne talked to Esteban about his father that morning, I thought about mine. I thought about handcuffs. I thought about fathers being taken away. I thought about uncles coming to the rescue and mothers gone.

The memory is mostly shadows now—my father's pale hands hanging from silver handcuffs. The cops pushing his head down into the police car. My uncle coming to me and lifting me up into his arms. I was three years old.

When my uncle first came to live with me, I was afraid. It was this vague fear around the edges of myself. Whenever I got real quiet in class, Ms. Laverne knew why. As I watched Esteban that morning, I felt it, the fear coming around the corner, finding me. Finding both of us.

I stared over at him. I wanted to give Esteban the *same* sign—my pinky pointing toward him while my thumb pointed toward me. I wanted to say, *I know that thing, Esteban. I've looked out the window that same way.*

Ms. Laverne turned from Esteban and told us to read quietly to ourselves. We took our books from our bags and opened them, but I don't know if any of us read a single word. The whole world felt wide open suddenly. Like it wanted to swallow us. I heard him tell Ms. Laverne, *I'm scared. I'm so, so scared.*

When the lunch bell rang, Esteban stayed behind. I wanted to touch his shoulder as I walked out and say, *It won't always feel like the first day. It won't always feel this bad.* But I didn't. I let the words hang in my throat until Holly grabbed my hand and pulled me down the hall with her.

Behind us, I heard Amari say, *E, what's going on? Talk to me, bruh.*

4

If there's one thing I *do* remember as clear as if it happened an hour ago, it's the afternoon when Ms. Laverne said to us, *Put down your pencils and come with me.* It was the end of September and we had been taking a spelling test. Esteban had been absent for days, and when he finally returned, Ms. Laverne asked him if he was up to doing some work and he nodded.

It helps me forget for a little while, he said.

Forget what? Amari asked.

That nobody knows where they took him. And now we're packing up everything, Esteban said. *Because if they took him, maybe they're going to take us too.*

I turned back to my test. I didn't want to think about fathers. Mine had been in prison for eight years by then.

In the last letter we'd gotten, he said he wasn't sure what would happen with his parole. If he got it, he didn't know exactly when he'd be coming home. I remember zero about living with him. Every good thing that happened had happened with my uncle. I couldn't imagine a different life. Didn't want to imagine it. Not for me. Not for anyone.

I was stuck on the word *holiday*. Did it have one *l* or two? My spelling had always been bad, but in Ms. Laverne's class it didn't matter so much because we were all at different levels in one thing or another. *The words you miss just tell me what you don't yet know,* Ms. Laverne always said. *It says nothing about who you are.* For some reason that made me feel better. I was eleven years old. What eleven-year-old didn't know how to spell *holliday*?

Put down your pencils and come with me.

The six of us stood up. Our school uniforms were white shirts and dark blue pants or skirts. We could wear any jackets, shoes and tights we wanted. I had worn blue-and-white-striped tights that day. Holly's tights had red stars on them. When we stood next to each other in the school yard that morning, our stars and stripes echoed the flag waving from the pole above us. We had spent the minutes before the bell rang dancing around it while

Holly sang that old song about having a hammer, *I'd hammer out danger, I'd hammer out a warning . . .*

We stood next to our desks and waited for Ms. Laverne to tell us what to do next. Amari pulled his hoodie over his head, then quickly pulled it off again, the way he sometimes did when he was nervous. Amari was beautiful. His skin was so dark, you could almost see the color blue running beneath it. His eyes were dark too. Dark like there was smoke behind his pupils. Dark and serious and . . . infinite. In that fifth/sixth grade class, I didn't know how to say any of this. I wanted only to look at him. And look at him.

Take a picture, it lasts longer, Amari said to me in such a cranky way, it almost brought me to tears. Ashton smirked, then pushed his hair away from his forehead and held his hand there.

She doesn't want a picture of you, Holly said. *Bad enough we have to look at you five days a week.* She had left her desk and was heading over to the classroom library.

Holly, back to your desk, Ms. Laverne said. *I want you all to take your books. You won't be coming back here today.*

We all gathered our stuff and followed her into the hallway.

Ms. Laverne took out her phone and said, *Smile, people.* In the photo, Holly and I have our fingers linked together, our tights looking crazier than anything. Amari has his hood halfway on and halfway off, and Tiago, Esteban and Ashton are all looking away from the camera. The picture is taped to my refrigerator now. We all look so young in it, our cheeks puffing out with baby fat, our uniform shirts untucked, Tiago's sneakers untied.

We walked down the hall behind Ms. Laverne, her heels softly clicking. I thought about how maybe one day I'd grow up to wear black shoes with small heels that clicked as I walked down a hall. And have students following behind who were a little bit in love with me.

Two small kids came running down the hall, but when they saw Ms. Laverne, they stopped and started walking so slowly, I almost laughed.

Esteban pulled his knapsack onto his shoulder and held it with both hands.

You okay, bro? Amari put his hand on Esteban's arm.

Nah, Esteban said. *Not really.*

Amari moved his arm over Esteban's shoulder. And kept it there.

5

When we got to Room 501, Ms. Laverne opened the door and held it for us. Nobody knew what to do, so we just walked in and stood there. The room was bright and smelled like it had just been cleaned with the same oil soap my uncle used on our floors. Back when me and Holly were in third grade, it had been the art room, but then someone gave our school enough money to open up a whole art studio in the basement, so now this was just a room we passed by sometimes and said to each other, *Remember when that used to be the art room?*

Welcome to Room 501, Ms. Laverne said.

Holly ran in ahead and the rest of us followed and looked around.

In the old art room, there were just a few of those

chairs with swing-up desks in a circle, a teacher's desk with no chair, a big clock on the wall and some little kid's ancient painting of a bright yellow sun thumbtacked to the closet door.

Esteban asked, *Are we getting transferred to a new class?* He put his knapsack down between his ankles and hugged himself.

Amari had taken his arm off Esteban's shoulder but was still standing close to him. When Esteban shivered, Amari put his arm back. I heard him whisper, *It's all good, bro. It's all good. Ms. Laverne's not taking us somewhere we don't want to be.*

Ms. Laverne sat on the edge of the teacher's desk and folded her arms. *Every Friday, from now until the end of the school year, the six of you will leave my classroom at two p.m. and come into Room 501. You'll sit in this circle and you'll talk. When the bell rings at three, you're free to go home.*

Why can't we just talk in our regular classroom? Holly asked, hopping up onto the teacher's desk. *I mean, in your classroom.*

Our regular classroom wasn't regular. We knew that. But still.

Down from there, please, Holly. Ms. Laverne waited for Holly to jump off again before she continued. *I don't want to hear what you have to say to each other. This is your time. Your world. Your room.*

Sounds like you're trying to get an early break from us, Holly said. *Give yourself your own kind of half day.*

Ms. Laverne laughed. *One day, Holly, your brain will be very useful to you.*

Holly looked like she wasn't sure if our teacher was complimenting her.

What I'm trying to do is give you the space to talk about the things kids talk about when no grown-ups are around. Don't you all have a world you want to be in that doesn't have people who look like me in it?

Nope, Amari said.

Yeah, Ashton said. *Not really.*

We like being with you, I added. *In the other room.*

You like what you know, Ms. Laverne said. *You like what's familiar.*

None of us said anything. She was right. What was wrong with liking familiar things?

Nothing's wrong with that, Ms. Laverne said, being a teacher/mind reader. *But what's unfamiliar shouldn't be scary. And it shouldn't be avoided either.*

But I don't know what we're even supposed to talk about, Tiago said. *Like, schoolwork and stuff? And to who?*

Schoolwork, toys, TV shows, me, yourselves—anything you want to talk about. To each other. And it's to whom, *Tiago.*

To whom, Tiago said to himself like he was practicing it. *To whom.*

I think any other bunch of kids would have started happy-dancing and acting crazy because there weren't going to be any grown-ups around. But we weren't any other kids.

I heard Amari say *that's stupid* so quietly that I wondered if I was hearing things. Then he said, *We could be talking in class if we wanted to be talking. You trying to change the art room into the A-R-T-T room—A Room To Talk.*

That's tight, Ashton said. He and Amari pounded fists. *I like that.*

Ms. Laverne clapped once and pointed at Amari. *You. Are. Brilliant.*

I could have come up with that. Holly rolled her eyes. *I could have added an* R *and thrown an acronym out there.* She said *acronym* loudly, making sure Ms. Laverne heard.

Nice use of the word, Holly, Ms. Laverne said. *Okay, so because the art room is now the A-R-T-T room, no one gets in trouble for talking here. You get in trouble for taking out your phone. You get in trouble for being disrespectful—*

How're you gonna know if you're not in here with us? Amari asked her.

I'll know.

And we all knew she was telling the truth. Teachers knew things. That's all there was to it.

Well, what if I don't have anything to say to anybody? Amari asked.

Ms. Laverne laughed again. *Since when do you not have anything to say, Amari?* She shook her head and waved her hand to include all of us. *I can't believe you all are so resistant. I'm giving you an* hour. *To chat! You get in trouble for this every single day. How many times do I have to say 'No talking'? Now I'm saying, 'Talk!'*

Amari tried to hide his smile but he didn't do a great job of it. *Okay . . . I'm vibing it. The old art room is the new A-R-T-T room, y'all.*

And I bet you can draw in here too, if you want, Ashton said to him.

Ms. Laverne nodded. *Draw, talk. And yes, Amari—the A-R-T-T room is beyond clever.*

Like I said, anybody could have thought of that, Holly said.

Yeah—but I see YOU didn't, Amari said.

And like I said, Ms. Laverne told us, *in this room we won't be unkind.*

She started it—

Doesn't matter, Amari.

I just want to get it straight, Ashton said. *So, school now ends at two o'clock on Fridays?*

He had pale white skin like my uncle, and hair that always fell into his eyes. Even as he asked, he was holding it back with his hand. Once Holly had said to him, *Just cut it already,* and his ears turned bright red. My own hair had always been bright red, but lately it had started getting darker and kinkier. If Holly's mother didn't braid it for me, I just pulled it back into a sloppy ponytail that frizzed all around my face.

Jeez, Ashton! Holly said. *That's not what she's saying. This is so not deep, people.*

I just don't really understand why we're going into another room, Ashton said, *by ourselves.*

I think, looking back on that day now, that's the line that will always stay with me—*another room, by ourselves.* How many other rooms by ourselves have we walked into since that day—even if they weren't real rooms and we didn't know that's what we were doing?

I stood there thinking about my father. In six months or a year—I didn't know exactly when—I'd be walking into another room, the one where my father lived with me. And as I stood there, Esteban was inside the room where he didn't know where his dad was. He glanced at me. That day, no one but Holly knew that my dad was in prison. I felt like I was betraying Esteban. Like I should have been standing next to him, saying, *Hey, it's gonna be okay.* But I couldn't. I couldn't tell the truth about my dad to help him. So I looked down at my skirt and thought about rooms. I wondered about Tiago, Holly, Amari and Ashton—what were the rooms for them? What did they hide inside those rooms? Another room, I thought. We are always entering another room.

That day, Ms. Laverne pushed us out—from the Familiar to the Unfamiliar.

It felt like an hour passed as she waited for us to say something. I looked at the clock. The second hand made an echoing sound when it ticked. It was five minutes past two. Fifty-five minutes left.

You can do this, Ashton. You all can do this, Ms. Laverne finally said. And with that, she walked away. With that, she let us go.

6

We stood around staring at each other. Holly took a seat and patted the one next to it. *Haley, sit here.*

The boys took the other seats.

Boys against girls is unfair, Holly whispered to me. *There's more of them. I've been saying this since school started. And plus—are we going to get tested on this?*

I smiled. Everything was unfair to Holly. We were both only children, but sometimes I thought maybe she had a bunch of brothers and sisters hidden away, because she always felt like someone was trying to cheat her out of something.

It's free time, I whispered back. *You heard Ms. Laverne. There's not going to be a test.*

Ashton, Tiago and Amari had pulled their seats farther back, making the circle bigger and lopsided.

Esteban's was next to mine. He sat down heavily, put his head on the arm of the desk and closed his eyes. His lips were chapped and he had tiny freckles over his nose that I hadn't noticed before.

I think that first day in the ARTT room, we were all sure his dad would be back soon. Tomorrow, the next day, the next week. None of us really knew about forevers yet. We were still just learning how things could change in a minute—how you could be in the middle of putting plates on the table when the phone rings with bad news. Or how your mother could come in and kiss you good night, and when you ask, *Is Papi home yet?* your mother says, *No, but maybe he's working late,* and then you wake up in the morning and run into the kitchen and your father's empty dinner plate is still on the table.

I thought about one of the stories my uncle liked to tell me. Before I went to sleep, he'd kiss my forehead and say, *Don't forget the happy ending.*

The story went like this: Two kids got lost in a forest. First they came to a snake and asked him the way to go. The snake said, *Freedom is through my lair.* The kids knew they'd get eaten if they followed the snake. They came to a spider and the spider said, *Freedom is in the center of my web.* They knew they'd get eaten there too. They came to a wolf, a grizzly, more snakes, and on and on it went. By the time they came to a wild boar, they were tired and hungry and scared. So when the wild boar said, *Freedom is inside that thicket of branches where I sleep,* they followed him. They had given up and figured it would be fast and maybe not as painful to get eaten by a wild boar. But instead, the wild boar fed them apples and honey. When their bellies were full and their eyes grew heavy, the wild boar covered them with blankets made of leaves stitched together with vines and watched over them while they slept. When morning came, they climbed on his back and he led them safely home.

When I asked my uncle what the moral of the story was, he said, *No moral. Just has a happy ending.*

Amari got up again and pulled his desk close to Esteban's. *Your pop'll come home, bruh,* he said. *I got a feeling.*

Back then, we still all believed in happy endings. None of us knew yet how many endings and beginnings one story could have.

7

One Saturday morning every other month, my uncle drove the two of us the seven hours to Malone, where my dad was in prison. On the first Saturday in October, my father refused to come down to the visiting room. My uncle and I waited. Time passed and my uncle paced and asked the guards what was happening. Finally, after I don't know how long, we got in the car and drove the seven hours back to Brooklyn.

On the ride home, I thought about how even our brains have rooms. And we could put stuff in those rooms we don't want to think about. Or remember. I decided I was going to put us sitting in that overheated waiting area into a room and lock the door.

But that night, when my uncle came in to tell me a story and kiss me good night, he said, *Your dad's afraid.*

He hasn't been on the outside in eight years. That's a long time.

But it's not our fault, I said. *The rule is every other month he sees us. And if he won't see us, how are we going to help him get ready for the outside? For coming home.*

My uncle sat on the edge of my bed. I was staring at the wall and wouldn't turn toward him. The anger inside me was fire. It was flames and ash too.

Look at me, my uncle said.

I shook my head. How could my father just sit in his cell. How could he choose sitting in a tiny cell over being in a room with us. With his brother. His daughter. His family. The only family he had left.

Haley, I'm serious, my uncle said. *Look at me.*

I turned toward him and pulled the covers up over my face.

Haley . . .

What! I snatched the covers below my chin and glared at him. *What do you want?*

My uncle's voice stayed calm. He pressed his pointer finger between my eyebrows. *I want you to know that we're all flawed,* he said. *We all have those days we just don't want to show up. Days we just want to forget the world. Doesn't make us bad people. Just makes us people.*

And time moves as it moves. In a month, this moment won't be anything.

But he didn't even want to see us. After we drove all the way up there. That's not right!

My uncle didn't say anything. My dad was his big brother. He always said that my dad had been his hero when they were kids, that he used to follow my dad everywhere.

He can't just choose to disappear. He can't just act like . . . like he doesn't love me. Like I'm not his daughter. He should be running to see me.

He does love you, Hales. The night you were born was the first time since we were kids that I saw my big brother cry. When I got to the hospital, you were asleep in your mom's arms. You had on one of those tiny blue-and-pink caps they put on newborns.

'Look at this,' your dad whispered. And he gently pulled the cap back to show me your bright red hair. You didn't have a whole lot then, and the room was nearly dark, but it glowed. I swear, your hair glowed.

No it didn't. I was trying to stay mad but I couldn't help smiling.

I swear, my uncle said. *You had glow-in-the-dark hair.*

Lies!

Anyway, your dad pulled the cap back over your head

while you and your mom kept on sleeping. Then he took my hand and pulled me out of the room.

I leaned my head against my uncle's chest. I could hear his heart. It was beating fast.

He said, 'She's so tiny, Steve. She's so perfect.' Then he put his hand over his face and started sobbing. 'Those two people in there, they're everything to me. Everything. How am I ever going to . . .'

My uncle stopped talking and sniffed. He reached his hand up to his face. I kept my ear pressed to his chest, my eyes closed. I knew he was crying and wanted to let him do it without getting embarrassed.

'. . . be the best dad and husband.' He asked me how he was going to be the best and I told him he didn't have to be the best. That nobody could be the best.

I could feel his chin nodding into my scalp. How many times had he told me this story? Still, I could listen to it for infinity.

I told him to just be there, my uncle said. *For everything. Every first word and step and first love.*

Yuck . . . , I said.

One day you'll fall in love.

Ixnay on the love, Uncle. Back to the story, please.

You know the story.

Still, I said. *I want to keep knowing it.*

My uncle's heart had slowed back down. Outside, a car drove past with its music turned up loud, the noise fading as it moved farther away.

Do you remember anything about her?

Just that picture, I said. *The one where it's the back of her and I can see her hand and her nails.*

My uncle was quiet for a long time. There had been a flood that ruined two computers' worth of pictures and a bunch of framed ones. And years later, just before the accident, there had been a small electrical fire that took out the bookshelves where all the photo albums and my uncle's record collection had been. The picture of my mom and dad had been in my father's wallet when he was arrested. The rest—that was up to memory.

She was so, so beautiful. My uncle pressed his lips into the top of my head. Then he pulled away and looked at me. *You look more like her every day, you know that?*

I nodded. *Yup. You keep saying so. But I look like you and my father too. I look like everybody.*

You look like you the most, though, Hales. I yawned as he brushed my hair away from my face with his hand.

Hey! I said. *Can you buy me a voice recorder? I need it for a project at school.*

How come you don't just use your phone? he asked.

Not allowed to.

Yeah. Sure. I can do that. You okay?

I nodded. *Yeah, just tired now.*

He kissed my forehead and turned out the light. *Good night, Haley. I love you to the moon.*

I yawned again, pulled the covers over my head and said, *I love you until Pluto becomes a planet again.*

8

The following Monday, right after dinner, my uncle put a recorder on the table. It was small enough to hold in my hand.

It's charged for now, he said. *But I can show you how to do it.* He looked at me. *By the way, what kind of school project is it?*

I don't really know what it is yet. It's like your stories.

How so?

I just want to record stuff, I told him. *And then I want to see what it becomes, you know? I want to be able to listen to it later and figure out what it is, I guess.* I turned the recorder around and around in my hands. *Thanks for getting this. Can I be excused, since it's your night for dishes?*

My uncle nodded, then frowned at me. *You okay?*

Yeah. I'm good.

I ran up the stairs to my room. The comforter on my bed had a purple unicorn on it. Once I had thought I was going to die if my uncle didn't buy it for me, and now, climbing onto it, it suddenly seemed silly and childish to me. How had what I liked changed that fast? I clicked the recorder on and held it in my lap. I recorded the sound of my own voice. *Testing, one, two, three. Testing, one, two, three,* then played it back. My voice sounded babyish and high. I got up, brushed my teeth and put on pajamas. Then I climbed into bed and turned the recorder on again.

My name is Haley Shondell McGrath. I am eleven years old. My father is in prison. My mother is dead. But don't feel sorry for me. I don't remember her. My uncle says I have her eyes. McGrath is an Irish name. It means 'Son of Grace.' But this McGrath right here is somebody's daughter.

Ms. Laverne has put the six of us in the ARTT room. We are going to go there every Friday for an hour to talk. Me, Amari, Ashton, Esteban, Holly and Tiago. Our story starts in Ms. Laverne's class in the borough of Brooklyn in the city of New York. But it's a story on top of a story.

It's a story that's started and ended a whole bunch of times. When we were studying the history of New York, we talked about the Lenape people—they were the real Native New Yorkers, but it wasn't called New York then. Their name for it was Lenapehoking. But then the Dutch settlers killed them and took their land. That means wherever we put a single foot—it's land that belonged to the Lenape. It's land they might be buried under. It's land that they died for. Ms. Laverne said that we should always remember this. That even though we have our dreams, the Lenape had dreams too. That even though we're here now, they were here first. I think this is what the world is—stories on top of stories, all the way back to the beginning of time. Ms. Laverne asked us if we were living in Lenapehoking, would we fight alongside the Lenape or would we try to take the land for ourselves? We all said we'd fight with them. We all said we'd try to help them hold on to their land.

I turned the recorder off. When we told Ms. Laverne we'd fight with the Lenape, she said, *But then maybe you wouldn't be here now? In America.* When she asked that question, none of us said anything for a while. We just all looked around at each other.

It wouldn't be America, but it would look like us,

Holly finally said. *It would look like this classroom, I think. Because we would figure out how not to just take something. And the Lenape people would probably share with us too . . .*

And then we'd all mix together, Tiago said.

Before Ms. Laverne talked about the Lenape, I hadn't really thought about the people who came here before we did. Indians were just Indians with big crowns of feathers, hopping around in circles and hitting their hands to their mouths. But after we learned about the Lenape, the Lenape *people*, I couldn't do that hand thing anymore. I couldn't see the people wearing their feathers at football games on TV and on Halloween and not think that's not right. That's not . . . not the truth. When I told Ms. Laverne that, she smiled and said, *Exactly.* Then she smiled even bigger and said, *I love this class SO MUCH!* Which made us all feel amazing.

I turned the recorder back on. *Ms. Laverne said every day we should ask ourselves, 'If the worst thing in the world happened, would I help protect someone else? Would I let myself be a harbor for someone who needs it?' Then she said, 'I want each of you to say to the other: I will harbor you.'*

I will harbor you.

||||||||||||||

Somewhere in the house, my uncle was playing his guitar. Beneath it, I could hear the soft hum of the dishwasher. He strummed the same chords over and over, then moved up the frets and strummed something different. The music trembled through the house. I stared at the wall across from my bed. The only thing on it was a painting of a dark brown girl sitting at a piano, her back to me, her arms spread across the keys. There was something about the shape of her shoulders that made me think of Esteban. Something both sad and . . . and proud at the same time. I pressed the cold metal of the recorder to my cheek and stared at the picture for a long time. One day, it too would be gone. The one time we took it down, there was a pale square behind it, as though the sun had tanned the wall around the painting. *And that,* my uncle said about it, *is all she wrote.*

Put the picture back, I had said to my uncle, turning away from it. *Now, please.*

Calm down, Hales. My uncle gave me a what's-the-big-deal look. *It's just a wall.*

But it was empty and I didn't want to believe that was all there was. That when one thing went away, just the pale ghost of it remained. I wanted to believe in stories on top of stories. Always something else. Always one more ending.

I put the recorder under my pillow. My hands were shaking. I knew Holly wouldn't have a problem with letting me record her. But I didn't know about the boys. One thing I wanted more than anything in the world was to hear what my mother sounded like. Was her voice high like mine? Did she have an accent? A lisp? I would never hear it again. Her voice was dust now. But if the others let me, I'd be able to keep a little part of us. I'd be able to keep *this* story. Forever.

9

The following Friday, we took our seats in the circle in the ARTT room. Amari took out his sketchpad. Ashton and the other guys started flipping through comic books, and me and Holly talked to each other. It was warm in the classroom. The school had turned the heat on and the tall radiators beneath the windows made soft hissing noises. We started peeling off our jackets and uniform sweaters. Even Esteban took off his Yankees jacket. Holly stood up and unbuttoned her school shirt. Underneath it she was wearing a gold T-shirt with the word MAGIC across the front.

You still have to wear your uniform, Amari said.

No I don't. Not here. Holly folded her shirt and put it in her backpack, then sat back down again.

Amari looked annoyed, like he wished he'd thought to wear a different shirt.

You're going to get Ms. Laverne in trouble.

Teachers can't get in trouble, Holly said. *They're like the God of school.*

Nah, the principal is the God. The teachers are the angels, Ashton said.

I had a teacher who was more like the devil once, Tiago said. *She was so mean! You couldn't even crack a joke! She'd just, like, yell at you, for not even doing anything bad.*

Ms. Laverne never yells, Holly said.

We all agreed.

But jeez, it's hot as the H-word in here, Holly said.

Amari said the H-word. *You can say it in here.*

Who wants to? Holly said. *I got smarter words. Anybody can curse.*

Before Amari could get mad, I took out the voice recorder.

Hey, guys. Can I ask you something?

Speak, Red, Amari said. Holly's mom had cornrowed my hair into a bun on the top of my head. I thought it looked less red when it was in cornrows, but I guess Amari didn't think so.

I explained to them about the recorder and played part of what I had recorded the night before.

It's like you're trying to remember us. Amari leaned back in his chair. *We're right here, though. But I guess like in an hour we won't be . . .*

And maybe next week we won't even be in this room again, like that kid that moved away who used to be in our class—remember him? Ashton added. He looked at me. *We don't have his voice anymore.*

That dude never talked! Amari said. *We never* had *his voice. If somebody asked me what he sounded like, I would be like, duh. You all remember his voice?*

The rest of us shook our heads.

I remember his curly hair, I said. *But that's not something you can listen to.*

Let me hear how I sound.

I turned the recorder on and Amari started trying to rap.

My name is A. Yeah. And that's okay. 'Cause around the way, it's like what's up what's up what's up, A?

Esteban looked like he was on the verge of laughing.

I played it back and then all of us were laughing. Amari's voice sounded off—too slow for rapping but too strange to be anything else.

It just needs some music behind it, Amari said. *You want me to sing?*

No! Holly said. *Please don't add more hot air to this*

already hot room. And plus, that's not what Haley is asking us, right?

I shrugged. I didn't think anything we said into the recorder was going to be wrong. It all was a part of us. I would have liked to hear what Amari sounded like when he sang.

It's for stories, Holly said, grabbing the recorder from me, turning it on and speaking into it. *It's for us getting remembered when we're not here anymore.*

It's for you not grabbing stuff out of people's hands, Amari said.

Holly handed the recorder back to me and didn't say anything. Sometimes her hands and mouth worked faster than her brain and made her say and do things she didn't really mean to do—like grab stuff. And say stuff.

I don't mind, I said to Amari, pressing the stop button. Because I didn't. Holly and I had been friends forever, and one thing about friends—they understood you.

I like that it's for memory. Esteban crossed his legs. He looked like the Buddha sitting there.

I held the recorder out to him, hopefully. *You want to try? You just push this button. Then you can tell the world about your dad. You can tell them your whole story.*

I don't know if I want to do that. Esteban pushed the recorder back at me.

My uncle says that when you tell stories, it's like letting out all the scared inside of you, I said. *It's like you help stuff make sense.*

Esteban looked down at the jacket he had draped over his lap. Then he started touching it gently, like he was remembering something about it.

It makes me too sad, he said. *I don't know if my papi is cold or hot or hungry or scared right now.* He took a deep breath. *I don't know anything. Nobody in my family does.*

But what about the stuff you do know, E? Amari asked. *If you talked about all the stuff you know . . .*

And things you remember from before, Ashton added. *Would that make it not so bad?*

Esteban shrugged.

A-R-T-T, Amari said. *A Room To Talk. We got you, E.*

Esteban reached out for the recorder. His nails were bitten so deep, there was a ring of pink skin at the top of his fingers. It looked painful. After a minute, he curled his fingers over the recorder and took it from me.

Okay, he said. *I think I do want to talk . . . about him. About my papi.*

10

We could ask you questions, like in interviews, Holly said.

Nah—that's dumb, Amari said. *Interviewers don't do it like that anymore, anyway.*

Yeah they do. Holly glared at him. *So who's dumb now. How else are they going to get people to talk?*

Amari leaned back and folded his arms and said in a deep voice, *So, Esteban, tell me about your dad. Give me the good, the bad and the ugly.*

Holly rolled her eyes. But before she could say anything else, Esteban started talking and I touched her hand to shush her.

We think they took my papi when he was coming home from work, Esteban said. *He works in a factory in Queens sealing video games in plastic. I don't know how he does it exactly, but he was going to show me. He promised me he was going to take me there one day, but he said it would have to be on a holiday because I couldn't miss school and he doesn't work on the weekends. My papi said weekends are always for the family and every day in school is a gift from God. He said that where he came from, I wouldn't be in school—I'd be working other people's land or in a factory. 'Imagine,' Papi said, 'a young boy like you with hands as hard as a man's.' He said since me and my sister were born in this country, we were born with the American Dream, like a silver spoon in our mouths. 'You're rich,' he always told us. Not in money, 'cause money isn't everything. But rich in dreams, 'cause in this country you can be anything.*

Esteban put his head down on the desk. I thought he was done and was going to take the recorder back when Amari spoke.

Now, Amari said, looking at Holly. *To go deeper in the story, you're supposed to ask him a question.*

Then you ask him a question, Mr. Smartypants, Holly said. *You're so up on the interview game, go for it.*

See? Amari said. *Why do I have to be the one to know everything. Yo, E.*

Esteban lifted his head again. *Yeah?*

Did your dad . . . Like, I know he works in a factory, but if he could be anything in the world, what would it be, you know? I'm not saying that there's anything wrong with working in a factory—

I know, Esteban said. *He used to say he wanted to be a poet like Pablo Neruda. That guy wrote a whole bunch of love poems that my papi would read to the family. And another guy named Pedro Mir. He was from the Dominican Republic like us. My papi said Pedro's poems were like the poems he wanted to write. They were about regular people and working and stuff like that. But you can't feed your family with a poem, my papi said. 'No se puede comprar un abrigo de invierno con un poema.'*

Tiago laughed. *I got you,* he said. *Oh man, that's like something my mom would say! 'You can't buy a winter coat with a poem.'*

Esteban put his hands in his pockets and pulled them inside out to show us the money you can't get from writing poetry. *My papi always says, 'I wrote poetry because of love. I stopped writing because of love too. Because I love my family.'*

Esteban got quiet again. In the hallway, some kids were dragging their sneakers across the floor and laughing about the squeaking sound. Holly put her fingers in her ears. An adult voice said, *Where are you supposed to be right now?*

The squeaking stopped and Esteban started talking again.

But my papi had another dream too. If you ever went to the park by the bridge on Sundays, you might have seen it. He can hit a baseball out of that park like nobody else. Everybody says so. They say, 'How can such a little man have so much power in his swing?' But he just pulls the bat back and WHAM! The ball goes flying and the guys in the outfield don't even run or lift their gloves in the air because they know that ball is gone. It keeps going and going like it wants to try to meet God. Then everybody starts cheering and jumping around Papi and telling him that he should be playing for the Yankees and pulling down the major dinero because, man, even A-Rod, who probably makes a million dollars, can't hit a ball like that. But my papi would just laugh. He said if you go to the Dominican Republic, you can find twenty more like him in the same park. He says like Pelé, they don't even have balls to play with, but they can hit rocks and cans and even once an old broken shoe, gone!

When he comes back, I want to see that, Amari said. *I need him to teach me.*

Esteban almost smiled. Then he didn't. *But what if he doesn't come back,* he said. *At night, when I'm dreaming, I dream that the Yankees recruited him and that's where he is. But then it's morning time and my mind is not dreaming so much anymore and the day is just like the day it was before—a day without my papi in it. And our apartment feels darker and more quiet. My little sister doesn't even cry when Mami tells her she can't watch television. She just climbs into Mami's lap and puts her thumb in her mouth.*

He's coming back, Tiago said.

I bet there's going to be a happy ending, Esteban, I said. *I bet he comes home and everything ends up fine.*

Yeah, Ashton said. *I bet by the time it's baseball weather—all of us are going to be sitting on the bleachers watching your dad hit that ball out the park.* He swung his arms back like he was batting, then shielded his eyes. *There it goes. There. It's gone!*

Esteban turned off the recorder and whispered, *Mami thinks that maybe they sent him back to the DR.*

None of us said anything. We didn't have to. We knew who the *they* people were. We knew what Esteban was afraid of. We knew why he turned off the recorder.

Mami says that if they sent him back, then even though we came here for the dream of America, we're going to have to go back too. Because without Papi, we're not a whole family. We're just like pieces of family. Like my little sister's wooden puzzle, the one that's supposed to be four puppies but it's only three and a half puppies now because the corner part that's the last puppy's neck and face and ears—that piece is gone. Papi is like the neck, face and ears of our family. When they took him, they took a little piece of all of us.

When Esteban handed me the recorder, I put it in my backpack. Then, without even thinking about it, I got back up and hugged him. It was a quick hug, but in that minute, I inhaled deep and he smelled like soap and cinnamon candy. I wanted to remember him—everything. I wanted to tell him that if he had to go away, I'd remember all the little things about him. But I didn't. I went back to my desk and stared down at my shoes.

Amari coughed the word *crush!* and everyone except me laughed.

Do you think it recorded the whole story, Esteban asked, *except for the part I didn't want to say in it?*

I nodded. *It's digital. It has a ton of memory. You can transfer the files to a computer and upload and stuff like that.* I realized how fast I was talking and stopped. Because now there was a sadness in the room like a thick gray ghost at my shoulder. I had been talking fast to cover it with words, send it hurling through the window, but I couldn't. I tried to imagine the ghost surrounded with sunlight and baseball games and poetry—good stuff that would push the ghost away.

When you talk, Esteban, Holly said, *it's like I can see everything you say. Your words draw pictures for me. I know that sounds crazy but they do.*

Esteban smiled.

That's what Papi says too. He says poems are tiny pictures.

I just hope you don't have to move away, Amari said. *It would just really suck.*

Both Tiago and Ashton said, *Yeah, it would.*

Esteban looked around at us like he was seeing us for the first time. His smile dipped down, then up again, then faded.

I know, he said. *But I want to be where my papi is. I want us to be a family again.*

11

It's like every day gives me something new to miss about my papi, Esteban said the week before Halloween. *There's all these holidays coming now.*

He left the circle and went over to the windowsill. Someone, maybe Ms. Laverne, had put pillows along the ledge, and bright sun was coming in. When he climbed up onto the ledge, he looked like a silhouette, like someone Amari could draw. Like someone who would make a beautiful painting. Amari took out his colored pencils and his sketchpad.

We heard that my papi's somewhere in Florida now, Esteban told us. *It's like a jail. But my papi didn't do anything bad. He was just working in the factory and they came and took him.*

Amari cursed and the word came out like a punch

against a wall. None of us said anything because we all wanted to curse or punch a wall too. The word was stuck in our hearts and throats and mouths.

But they'll let him go, won't they? Ashton said. *I mean, they can't just take people away like that. And keep them! That's just all kinds of unfair, bro.*

Wake up, Ashton. Amari didn't look up from his drawing as he spoke. *This is America. Supposed to be the land of the free, but we free? Nah. We got rules everywhere we step. No running, no cursing, no playing, no yelling, no staying up late, no this and no that. Now, grown-ups, they're the free ones. And if it's not grown-ups all up and down our backs, it's teachers—*

Not Ms. Laverne, Holly said.

Amari flicked his hand into the air, his eyes rolling up to the ceiling. *She put us here,* he said. *She didn't say, 'You all want to come to the art room?' She said, 'Y'all going to the art room.' That's freedom? That's power?*

We got freedom. Holly glared at him. *It's not like before when we couldn't swim in pools or go to stores and stuff because we were black or something. It's not segregation.*

Nope, Amari said. *It's not. So we should stand up and cheer for America, I guess.* He rolled his eyes again.

We can live anywhere we want—

You *could live anywhere* you *want,* he said. *You're a rich girl, Holly. Can Tiago live anywhere? Can Ashton live in Connecticut anymore?*

Yeah I can, Ashton said.

How?

Ashton shrugged. *Just move back. We could just move back someday.*

With what money?

Ashton looked down at his desk and didn't say anything.

Nah, Tiago said. *Amari's right. We're not so free.*

Can't even walk around with your hood on if you want, Amari said. *And even here! We got uniforms! That's free?*

No one said anything.

Yeah, Amari said, answering his own question. *Didn't think so.* He went back to his drawing. When I leaned over to look, I could see that most of the paper was covered with colorful guns—blue ones, green ones, yellow ones.

Why are you drawing those?

Amari looked at me like he was surprised I was there. *Why are* you *so nosy, Red?* He covered more of the paper with his arm and kept on drawing.

Hey, Amari. My friend asked why are you drawing guns, Holly said. *And you know her name.*

It's just a picture, Esteban said. *A picture can't hurt you. It's like the same thing as a poem. But not in words.*

Amari held up the piece of paper and aimed it at Holly. *Pow. Mind your business. Now, those are words to go with my picture.*

I'm going to tell Ms. Laverne you're up in here threatening people, Holly said.

Amari looked sadder than anything for a minute, like if someone touched his shoulder, he'd start to cry. But then, just like that, his face went back to normal. He held up the paper, aimed it at Holly again and dropped his voice down to a creepy whisper.

Can't tell anybody anything. We. Are. All. Alone. Now. I guess that means we're free.

Even Holly couldn't think of anything to say to that.

12

The next day, I received a letter from my father.

I stood shivering in front of our mailbox, staring at the long envelope—my father's name, prison address and number in the upper left-hand corner, my own name and address in my father's curling handwriting across the middle. I stood on our stoop and stared up the block. Two men were walking a gray dog. One said something and the other threw his head back and laughed. They were too far away for me to hear the laughter, but I could see it. Their faces seemed so happy. So free.

I thought about what Amari had said the day before, about how none of us are really free, then looked down at the letter again. I had known my dad before he went to prison but didn't remember any of it. Did he ever tickle me? Throw me into the air and catch me? Did he ever push me on a swing in the park or talk me through a tantrum? When I remembered those things, it was always my uncle I saw. I put the envelope against my nose and sniffed it. His letters always smelled like prison—like bleached floors and the vague hint of sour milk.

My uncle was in the city, playing music with some friends of his from college. When I got back inside, the house felt too quiet. Too empty. I sat in the window seat and held the envelope in both hands, turning it over and over. Outside, the leaves on the tree started blowing, silently, like the man's laughter. They had long ago turned brown, and above them, the sky was incredibly blue. I don't know how long I stared up at it before finally opening my father's letter. I was afraid. I think something inside my heart broke when he didn't come down for us when we last visited. Something I didn't even know was breakable just fell apart inside me.

Dear Haley,

I'm sorry I didn't show up last time. I will never not show up for you again. Not while I'm here inside. Not when I'm on the outside again. I know you have so many questions for me. One day I hope to be sitting at a table across from you. No inmates and guards around us, no noisy television, no cold gray room, no intercom blasting names and demands and rules. For as long as you could talk, Haley, you've only known me as a prisoner. I look forward to the day when that's no longer who I am to you.

Love,

Your Father

I got to the end of the letter and went back to the beginning. *I'm sorry I didn't show up . . .*

Love, Your Father.

I did love him. I'd only ever really known him in his prison uniform. And inside those gray rooms. I'd only ever really known how hard he hugged me, how his eyes got bright when he saw us standing there. How it always looked like he wanted to laugh and cry at the same time.

Love your father. No matter what, my uncle always said. *You love your father.*

I folded the letter back into its envelope, ran my fingers over my name. My father's hand had written those letters. He had sat in his cell, bent over the page and wrote those words. *I'm sorry . . .*

Forgive and forget, my uncle said. Staring at those

letters, I thought I could forgive my father. But I could never forget. I'd lock every moment of memory inside a room in my brain and hope they'd multiply like cells in our bodies, until I was a grown-up all filled with memories. Maybe that's what made us free. Maybe it was our memories. The stuff we survived, the good stuff and the bad stuff.

I climbed the stairs slowly, the third one creaking, the fifth one slanting downward. From memory I knew how my feet would land on each stair. I knew how my door would whine as I closed it. I knew the water rattling through the pipes when my uncle showered and how the dog in the backyard across from ours barked every morning when its owner let it out. Everything around me was as familiar as my purple comforter, as easy as saying my own name. I sniffed the letter again before putting it in the drawer with the others, then lay down on my bed and wrapped my comforter around me.

13

Think about the Familiar. Every morning, you get up. You brush your teeth and wash your face and put on the clothes you'll be wearing that day. Days roll into weeks and weeks turn into months. The leaves start falling from the trees. A wind comes from the north and makes you shiver so hard, your teeth chatter. Every morning, you eat breakfast at school with your friends. You tear into the bagels and slurp up cereal and side-eye the suspicious-looking eggs. You and your friends laugh over silly stuff—Tiago's Santa hat with the white beard attached and the silly faces he makes whenever he wears it, Amari's drawings of dogs with wings, cats with crutches, impossible ice cream sundaes like wishes on paper.

Think about what you know—how the mornings always come too quickly and the weekends don't last long enough. How your uncle has always shaved the left side of his face before the right—for good luck, from habit. The Familiar.

The trips to Malone, Taco Tuesday, stories at night, hair day at Holly's house. The Familiar.

A lady with a tiny black dog leaves her building every morning just as you're leaving yours and she waves and you wave. But that's the only time you've ever seen her.

We knew what we knew. We did what we had always done. Then one day, Ms. Laverne said,

Put down your pencils and come with me.

We left our classroom and walked down the hall to the art room. The Familiar popped like a bubble above our heads. But we held tight to our knapsacks and kept on walking.

14

For the two weeks after Halloween, we snuck our candy into the ARTT room, trading and sharing it until our stomachs twisted up from too much chocolate and our tongues burned from Sour Patch Kids and Jolly Ranchers.

The half-moons beneath Esteban's eyes grew darker, and some days his uniform looked like he'd slept in it. He had left the circle completely, sitting on the windowsill and staring out into the school yard.

One Friday, just as we entered the ARTT room, without saying a word, Ashton and Amari started moving our desks. They arranged them around Esteban at the window. None of us said anything, but Esteban looked up. Then he smiled.

We took our seats in the new circle like it was just a

regular Friday. But the circle was a little smaller now, our chairs closer together. *We* were closer together.

Amari pulled out his sketchbook and started drawing. Then, just as quickly, he snapped it shut.

Hey, Red. Can I talk into your recorder? I got something I want to say.

Sure.

I nearly spilled out my whole knapsack rushing to get the recorder for Amari. When I handed it to him, he turned it around and around in his hand. *It's the button on top that starts recording me, right?*

I nodded.

My name's Amari, he rapped. *Rhymes with* Atari. *I'm old-school like that. I'm so smooth like that.*

Oh man, Holly said. *You are not going to spit weak raps into history, are you?*

Amari looked like he was ready to say something back to her, then he sat up, his lips pressing together.

Wait a minute, he said slowly. *Twenty years, we all meet back in this room and you can play this for us. My voice is already changing, so let me catch it like it is.* He smiled.

Your voice is SO not changing, Holly said. *Keep dreaming.*

Amari rolled his eyes at her. *Jealous. That's all you are.*

Nope. Believe it or not, I don't want my voice to change. Sweet and fine the way it is.

The other guys smiled, but Amari just looked at Holly. She stared right back.

Why don't you two get married and get it over with, Ashton said.

Both Amari and Holly made gagging sounds, but my stomach double-flipped and landed. Hard. No. They hated each other. No, Ashton was wrong. But then I saw the edges of Holly's lips turn up.

Whatever, Amari said, turning back to me. *If it was cool with Esteban, I'm good. Just don't play it for nobody but us. Twenty years from now, we all meet right back here in this room. The six of us.*

That would be cool, Tiago said.

Yeah, Esteban agreed. *That would be nice. We'd be old, though.*

Red's gonna be the first one I recognize, Amari said.

I smiled. Twenty years seemed like a hundred years. I couldn't even imagine a room without the six of us in it. One day, we wouldn't be in Ms. Laverne's class. But Amari would recognize me.

Esteban had stopped smiling. So had the others.

It's strange to imagine us not together anymore, Ashton said. *I know it hasn't been that long, but . . .*

Yeah, but still, Amari said.

So let's make it a promise! Holly slapped both hands down on the arm of the desk. *Twenty years from now, no matter where we're living, no matter what. We'll meet back here in the ARTT room.*

Kick any little kids in here out, Ashton said. *Because we were here first!*

Amari held up the recorder. *And Red will bring this and we'll all listen to ourselves.*

I nodded.

The green light on the recorder was still on. *It's recording us,* I said.

That's cool, Amari said. *You think you can hold on to this thing for twenty years?*

Yeah, I said.

It sounds corny, Ashton said. *But it sounds really cool too, because mostly, when you move away from someplace, you don't see the people again and you don't even remember what they sound like.*

He got quiet, looked down into his lap and sighed. It was such a deep and heartbreaking sound. A sound I knew wouldn't sound any less sad over the years. A sound I'd hear again and again and remember Ashton, his head down, his hair falling over his forehead, his cheeks puffing out, his lips parting to exhale air.

15

Amari rested the recorder on top of his drawing pad. Then he pulled a green marker from his pack and started tracing it. His hand moving slow and sure around the recorder. *I think what's really messed up is the way everything changes all quick from one year to the next. You know?*

Like, I don't mind my voice getting deep. He stopped drawing and looked up at Holly. *Even if you don't hear it, it is!*

But it's like one day you asking for some Batman sheets for your bed, and the next day somebody telling you Batman is for babies. Stuff like that.

I thought about the way I had once loved purple so much. About how deeply I had once believed in unicorns.

And like hugging and stuff, Amari said. *Boys don't*

hug each other. I mean, when you're little, you do. It's okay then. You always see the kindergarten kids running to each other and hugging like they haven't been together in years. That's what I love about little kids—they just get to be little kids. But when you get to be big—like us—all that goes away. It goes far away. Like once with my dad. I was about eight years old and I went running to him ready to jump in his arms like I always did and he said, 'Whoa, big man! You too grown for that now.' One day yes. Next day no.

But you know, deep . . . like way down inside me? I want it back sometimes. I want to hug you, Esteban, like Red hugged you, and say, 'That sucks, bruh!' I want to promise you your dad'll be back soon and that this was just a glitch in the road.

That's what my dad called this moment we're living in. 'Glitch in the road.' The Saturday before last, he wouldn't let me go anywhere. Not to Ashton's house. Not to the corner store. Not even to the stoop to hang out with my boys on the block. He kept saying, 'You just sit tight, Amari, and watch all the TV you want. I'm gonna talk to you later.'

Amari looked up at us. *All the TV I want?!?! That was like a zombie talking. Because my dad is the king of*

'Turn off the TV and read a book.' My dad is the 'I'll throw that TV out the window' kinda dad. You get the picture?

We all nodded.

So around one o'clock, in the middle of me watching like my hundredth TV show, my dad came in and said, 'Walk me to the bank, Mar.' That's his nickname for me. I found out it means 'Sea' in Spanish.

Mar, Tiago and Esteban said with an accent.

Mar, the rest of us said softly.

He just calls me Mar because it's short for Amari, but I like that the short name has a meaning. Amari means 'Strength' if you use the Yoruba translation. But in Japanese it means 'Not Really.' I think if we were Japanese, I'd be real mad about my name. Just saying.

Not Really, Esteban said. *That's crazy. But funny.*

Hey, Not Really, Ashton said. *Clean up your room because it's not really clean right now.*

The rest of us laughed.

That's what's up, Amari said. *But the cool thing is, that's not the translation, so everybody can let it go now.*

I guess we can, Holly said. *But . . . Not Really.*

Even Amari smiled and started talking again. Maybe in twenty years he'd be the mayor of New York and we'd all be in the audience listening to him talk. He spoke like he was so sure of everything he said. Like all his life someone had been saying, *You're right, Amari. You're smart, Amari. You're beautiful, Amari.*

So my mom was at a spin class with her 'girls,' he said, holding up quotation fingers. *They're grown ladies, but she always calls them her 'girls.' Every Saturday they go to a spin class to work off the calories, and then they do brunch. I don't get it. That's all I'm saying. Why go sit on a bike for hours, then go eat pancakes and sausage and eggs and bacon and everything on a menu? That's crazy! Just go eat! That's what I do the Saturdays I have brunch with them.*

And you know what else is crazy, Ashton said. *How come grown-ups always tell each other how young they look, and kids always want to be grown-up already, so we lie and say we're ten when we're really nine or that we're thirteen when we're really twelve?*

But grown-ups lie too, Amari said.

Facts, Tiago said. *My mom's been thirty for, like, ten years!*

Mine too, Holly said. *And don't let her see some gray hairs. It's like she's seen a ghost—all screaming and whatnot. Then running around the house looking for tweezers to pluck it out.*

Wrinkles too. Ashton laughed. *My mom is like, 'Oh*

my God, Ashton, please tell me you can't see this wrinkle by my chin.' And of course I can see it—it's, like, the size of a river. But I just go, 'Uh-uh, I don't see anything.'

You know that's the right *move,* Amari said. *Or else!*

Everyone nodded. I didn't know anything about mothers and wrinkles, but I knew that when my uncle first saw some gray hair on his head, he went into his room, closed the door and played sad songs on his guitar for hours.

Anyway, Amari said, *me and my dad started walking to the bank. And he goes to me, 'Look, Mar. I want to talk straight with you.'*

And I was like, 'Yeah?' Because that was strange. I mean, me and my dad, we always just talk straight. Nothing crooked about it.

So he says to me, 'You're in fifth grade now. Happened so fast, I didn't even see it coming.'

And I had to smile when he said that. It has to be at least two years since I last sat in his lap.

Then my dad said, 'This country is going a little bit crazy. I know it's just a glitch in the road, but I want you to know there're things you can't do anymore.'

And I'm like, 'What kind of stuff,' because I had thought the older you got the more stuff you can do, not can't.

He said, 'You can't be running around the playground

with that water gun, for one. Or that Nerf gun, or that little light-up key-ring gun thing you got from your aunt last year? You can't even carry that in your pocket anymore.'

Then my dad goes, 'You get me, right, Mar?'

And I just nodded. I was so mad, I didn't even look at him.

Amari looked around at us. I knew what he was talking about. I'd seen the papers and heard Holly's mom and dad talking about a boy who got killed for playing with a toy gun. Holly's mom said that it wouldn't have happened if the boy was white, and Holly's dad had nodded.

The cops who shot that kid in the park didn't even ask him any questions, Amari said. *Just came in the park and shot him right away. And then when his big sister tried to run to him, they didn't even let her go to him.*

How come they didn't let her? Ashton looked surprised, like maybe this was his first time hearing the story.

Amari shrugged. *I don't even know,* he said. *It's crazy. My sister's seventeen, she would lose her mind if anyone ever even looked at me funny. That's how crazy she is about me. When I heard about that boy and his sister, it made something in me twist up. Made me want to punch a wall or even worse. That boy could have been me or Esteban or Tiago . . .*

Or me, Ashton said.

Amari didn't say anything to Ashton. He acted like he hadn't heard him and kept talking.

My mom never liked me playing with guns anyway, Amari continued. *So I knew my days of playing with them were numbered. But I didn't know it would all come this quick. You know, like with the hugs. Felt like I woke up one day and it was just corny to do. But playing with my guns wasn't corny yet. A water-gun fight on a hot day is still the best thing ever.*

Facts, Tiago said. *When you're all hot and somebody comes out of nowhere and starts squirting you? You act mad, but son, I gotta say, that's the best, bro.*

For real. Amari pounded Tiago's fist.

And that Nerf gun you got, A? Amari said. *The one that shoots, like, fifty feet. That's power.*

Yeah, Ashton said. *Remember when we were shooting the dead leaves off the trees?*

Amari nodded. *We were like, powpowpow!*

Some serious sharpshooting, Ashton said.

They both got quiet. I could tell by their faces that they were back in the park with their Nerf guns, aiming them at the trees.

No disrespect to you, Ashton, but it sort of sucks that you can still go to the park with that gun and not have to worry about getting killed.

It's okay, Ashton said. But he started biting on his bottom lip.

I can't stand guns, Holly said. *I never saw one in real life and never want to.*

Nobody's talking about real guns! Amari said. Then he looked at Ashton. *Ashton, you're, like, one of my best friends, you know that, right?*

Ashton nodded. *Same.*

But that kid getting killed and then my dad saying I couldn't play with guns anymore? That made me hate you.

But I didn't do—

Not YOU, I mean, I didn't hate you. I don't know how to say it.

I do, I said. *It's not fair. It's not fair that you're a boy and Ashton's a boy and he can do something you can't do anymore. That's not freedom.*

Amari nodded. *Yeah to what Red's saying. You can just play with your Nerf gun all you want, anywhere you want, and no cop is gonna run up and shoot you.*

Amari stopped talking. He got up and walked over to the window, taking the recorder with him. Then, in slow motion, he made the hand that wasn't holding it into a gun, straightened his arm and aimed outside.

The cops shot that boy in the stomach, he said. *With real bullets. Not soft ones that bounce off. And the boy fell in the playground. And then he died.*

Amari kept his gun hand pointed at the window, his voice dropping down low. *And maybe if it was a windy day, the swings just kept on swinging. Making that sad, whiny sound that swings make when they're still moving and nobody's on them. And that boy should have been running and playing and jumping off those swings. Whenever I jump off a swing, it feels like I'm flying. It feels like I'm more free than anything. That boy should have been having that feeling. He shouldn't have been feeling like he was dying. He should have been feeling like he was free.*

16

It was 3:15 and we could hear the kids moving through the hall and leaving school, but none of us moved. Then the halls got quiet. It felt like we were the only ones left in the building.

Ashton was looking down at his hands.

Amari gave me back the recorder and started putting his drawing pad and pens back into his knapsack. I slid the recorder into mine.

The door squealed open and Ms. Laverne came in. She had this small smile—that grown-up smile that says, *See, I knew this was the right thing.* But then she saw that none of us were smiling.

All okay? she asked.

We didn't say anything at first. Then Amari said,

We're good. We were just finishing up. He sounded like a grown-up.

Okay . . . Ms. Laverne looked a little confused. *Be out of here by three thirty at the latest and have a great weekend.*

We all said goodbye to her and waited until the door clicked shut.

I think your dad's being unfair, Ashton said. *It's just playing. And plus, the Nerf guns are orange, so it's not like they look real or anything.*

The kid that got killed had a toy gun, Amari said. *My pops said it's like we're suspects from the day we're born.*

Amari and Ashton looked at each other, both of them mad.

Yeah, Holly said. *And what about all the other kids we don't even see on the news. Like my cousin who got stopped on his bike and handcuffed. And he's only thirteen. He was just riding his bike. But the cops said he fit the description of another kid on a bike. How many black kids ride bikes? Lots!*

Something like that happened to my cousin Jonathan, Tiago said. *He lives in the Bronx and this cop just pushed him when he was hanging out with his boys. They were hanging by those mansions up by Van Cortlandt Park.*

And the cop said they didn't live there, but one of his friends did. Plus that cop said they were being loud, but they're teenagers, so duh.

Yeah, Holly said. *Show me some quiet teenagers.*

And what about that guy with asthma that they choked, Amari said. *And that other guy who got beat up by a bunch of cops and nobody would have known about it if somebody hadn't recorded it on their phone.*

It could happen to anybody, Ashton said. *Not just . . . like black guys and Puerto Rican guys.*

Amari stood there looking at Ashton for a minute. Then he just shook his head and put his backpack on his shoulder.

Show me one time when it was somebody who looked like you, Ashton.

I still think—, Ashton started to say. Amari didn't wait for him to finish, though. Just left without even waving goodbye.

17

The Familiar. You walk the land you've always known. The river, the ocean, the deep forest belong to you. This is Lenapehoking. This is your home. You know the print of every animal moving through the dirt—deer, raccoon, rabbit, bear. You know the scent of pine and the many ways root bark can heal.

Then one day, there's a ship on the water. And then another. And another. You learn quickly that the men on board aren't kind. Behind you, children play a game involving small stones. Behind you, your mother and your grandmother scrape an animal hide clean, then hang it to dry in the sun. A baby sleeps shaded inside his cradle-board, hanging from a tree.

You watch, listen to the stories the women tell each

other, the way their gossip lifts up into the wind and moves through this land. This land that's your land.

Then men come closer. And raise their guns. For a long time, these people's stories will bury yours.

Would you harbor me?

Who would you have harbored? Ms. Laverne asked us.

I thought of this as Amari left the classroom with his knapsack on his shoulder and Ashton looked down at his hands.

18

That afternoon, Holly's mom, Kira, picked us up from school. She was talking on her phone as we climbed into the car, her braids hanging down over the back of her seat.

Did you get—? Holly started asking, and her mom held up my sleepover bag, then put her finger to her lips.

So many times, I'd stared at Kira, wondering if my own mom had looked like her. The one picture I had of her showed my mom and dad walking away from someone's car. My mother in a long white coat and hat, and my father in a T-shirt and jeans. Her hand was trailing back behind her and I could see her fingers—long and dark brown, the nails painted bright red.

How many times had me and Holly painted our nails? A hundred? A thousand? And each time I held my hand out, I wanted it to transform into the bright red and brown of my mother's hand. Every. Single. Time.

But I never could. In the fall, my skin started fading back to a lighter brown, blue veins showing on the inside of my arms. But in the summer, it darkened so much that strangers asked, *What are you?* A question I hated. *Tell them you're a human,* Holly always said. *And then ask them what are they?*

What good happened today? Kira asked when she finally hung up her cell and got ready to drive.

Nothing, Holly said before I could even open my mouth. *Can we get pizza?*

Out the window, I saw Ashton walking by himself, his hands shoved way down in his pockets. An older boy approached him and slapped the back of Ashton's neck. Then another boy did the same thing. And another. All of them were laughing. I watched Ashton sink further down into himself, his eyebrows furrowing as he tried to swat the hands away. I wanted to jump out of the car and run over, but we were already pulling away from the curb. When he got to the corner, Ashton started running. Maybe he ran all the way home.

Did you see that, I asked Holly.

See what?

Nothing.

And can we get the pizza from the place on Nostrand? Holly said to her mom. *I don't like that other place. You and Dad do, but I don't.* After a minute she said, *Haley doesn't either.*

I'm good either way, I said, still looking out the window.

It's called *necking*. In the olden days, necking meant "kissing," but not anymore. Now it meant running up to someone and slapping their neck. Hard. How did the same word that described two people in love become a word that described something so mean?

Now I remembered some mornings when Ashton came into class, his neck so red, it looked like sunburn.

And I get to choose the movie, Holly was saying. *Something good this time.*

No R ratings, her mother said. *And no trying to sneak in an R rating after I'm asleep.*

The Familiar. You plan what movie you're going to watch. You pull your collar up to hide the pain showing on your neck. You sit staring out a window, remembering your papi. You pack your Nerf guns away—maybe forever. You walk into the Unfamiliar.

We drove by brownstones and apartment buildings. Signs in the corner bodega window said WE ACCEPT EBT and ATM INSIDE. The Familiar.

There weren't a lot of white kids at our school. There were some little ones in kindergarten and first and second grade, but not in fifth and sixth. Ashton was the only white kid in our room. Unless you counted half of me.

I'm cooking tonight, Kira said. *And we need to get to work on Haley's hair.*

I looked up in time to see Holly roll her eyes. *Her hair looks fine to me, Ma.*

But we both knew she was lying just so we could get to the movie part of the night faster. The one thing my uncle never mastered was my hair. Even though the red came from my father, the curls and kink came from my mom. My uncle had watched videos about kinky hair and bought products that were supposed to make it easy to comb through. He'd learned that a fine-tooth comb was never going to make its way through my hair and that a wide-toothed one really only worked when my hair was wet. When I was five he had a black girlfriend for about three months, and I swear they broke up because she couldn't help him with my hair. Looking back on that, I remember the woman had a nearly shaved head, which should have been a sign to him that hair wasn't her specialty.

Then one day, after me and Holly had become friends, Kira walked over to my uncle in the school yard.

I can help you with your daughter's hair, she said. Holly was standing beside her, her hair neatly braided into cornrows.

That's her uncle, Ma, Holly said. *Not her dad.*

And that was the beginning of me spending most Friday nights at Holly's house. Sometimes my uncle went out on dates those nights. When I was little, I was so afraid he'd fall in love with someone and leave me. Or worse, move them in and they'd try to become my mother. But that never happened. And now I don't feel that way. Some days, seeing the loneliness in my uncle's face, hearing him play his sad love songs on the guitar, watching the way he looked at other couples on the street, I wanted him to fall in love. I wanted him to find a happy ending.

You okay? Kira asked me through the rearview mirror. She looked worried.

I'm good. I smiled at her.

Why wouldn't you be? Holly said, suddenly reaching over and hugging me hard. *It's Friday!*

Yassssss! we said together. Like we'd done so many Fridays before.

I got a new nail polish for us to try, Holly said. *It's called Royal Ruby.*

Cool, I said. Maybe that would be the one.

19

The day my uncle told me how my mother died, I was six years old.

It was winter and we were in a park. There was a covered slide that wound around like a snake, sending kids flying through a dark tunnel. Lots of kids landed so hard, their parents carried them away in tears. But not me. I loved everything about that slide—the steep metal stairs that led to the top of it. The way you had to stand above it so that you could slip yourself in legs first. The way your body seemed to get snatched away, pulled through the darkness, then back into the bright light of winter.

My uncle calls it the One Time—the way you can do something again and again and again, and then the One Time, something goes all kinds of wrong. I had climbed to the top of the slide and slid my legs through. The tunnel sucked me into its darkness and I happy-screamed my way to the bottom. The park was nearly empty, but that day, as I sailed through the tunnel, another kid raced toward the slide on a scooter. He was a big kid and thick as a wall. My uncle saw it before I did—the kid coming toward the slide, me speeding through, then coming out into the light just as the kid sped past. We landed in a pile of banging heads, cracking bone and blood. Through the pain, dizziness and my own screaming, I could hear my uncle calling my name, telling me to stay awake. His voice was deep and ragged and filled with so much sadness, it registered through my pain. But then my uncle wasn't calling my name. He was calling out to Berry. *Berry,* he said. *Berry. Please be okay.*

Berry was my mother's name. Short for Beryl. Short for Beryl Lee. Then my uncle was untangling me from the mess of screaming boy and spinning wheels. Through the haze of everything, I could see surprised looks on people's faces. I could hear the boy crying. Could see a woman kneeling down to hug him.

You're good, Berry, my uncle said again and again. *You're going to live. You're going to be okay.* It was my first and only time in an ambulance. I don't know how it got there, but I was inside of it, the sirens blaring, my uncle's ragged voice, the bright lights and someone else—a paramedic maybe—moving around us. On the way to the hospital, I tried to tell him I wasn't Berry, but the pain in my arm and head made it too hard to form words, and somewhere between the park and the hospital, I must have passed out.

When I woke up, I was in a hospital room and it was dark out. My arm was in a cast from shoulder to wrist and there was a thick bandage over my ear.

Sixteen stitches behind your ear, my uncle said, bending forward to kiss the top of my head. *You're a soldier in the army of sliding board catastrophes.*

I'm not Berry, I said. It hurt to talk. The words pounded against my head.

My uncle leaned closer. *You're not very what, sweetie?*

No, I said, my words coming quiet and slow. *I'm not Berry. You. You called me Berry before.* The cast was heavy and tight. There were lights flashing on the wall and doctors being paged over an intercom. The room smelled like the alcohol prep pads my uncle kept in the medicine cabinet. *You called me Berry,* I said. *But I'm Haley.*

My uncle was sitting in a chair right next to me. He leaned back and blinked until tears appeared. He wiped them away with his other hand, then blinked again.

Beryl, he said. *That's what we called Beryl.*

My mom? I tried to sit up but it felt like somebody's huge hand was pushing me back down.

He kissed the top of my head again, then leaned his cheek against it. *I was so scared,* he said. *I was scared like I was the night she died.*

My uncle and I had two rules. No lying. No dodging. If either one of us asked a question, the rule was the other person had to answer it. They couldn't try to dodge around it or change the subject. *That's how wars happen,* my uncle said. And family wars too.

How did she die? I asked.

A car accident, my uncle said. *When you were three. You don't remember any of it?* He sounded surprised.

I remember she would sing to me, I said. *A song about summertime.*

My uncle got quiet. He had been gently rubbing my head, but he stopped. I wanted him to keep doing it.

It was a song about summertime, I said again. I was sleepy and my head was hurting again. *Am I going to have to sleep here?*

Just tonight, my uncle said. He was sounding choky again.

My mouth was hot and dry. My uncle got me a glass

of water and helped me take a few small sips. The pain shooting through my arm hurt like crazy, hot and sharp as a flame.

That big kid broke my clothes and my arm, I said.

He didn't mean it.

I know.

We listened to the hospital sounds without saying anything. Somebody was calling for Doctor Somebody. A kid was crying somewhere. A nurse ran past my room.

Will my dad always be in prison? I asked sleepily.

Not always.

But when he comes home, can I still live with you?

We got time to figure it all out, Hales.

I pulled his hand back to my head. He rubbed it until I fell asleep.

20

By mid November, it had gotten colder. The school cranked the heat up a notch and the radiator's hissing got louder. We were all sweating, but Ashton kept the scarf he'd been wearing all day wrapped around his neck. The day before, he'd worn a turtleneck under his uniform shirt. He had moved his desk and was sitting outside the circle, far away from Amari. But they kept looking at each other like there was something they wanted to say. And couldn't.

I took out my recorder and started to turn it on.

I don't want you recording me, Ashton said.

Then don't say anything, Holly said before I could talk. The week before, she had brought her knitting needles and a ball of purple yarn to school. She sat there, the needles clicking over themselves, the purple square of yarn growing more rectangular. Her grandmother had taught her to knit before she died. I'd only met her once. She was tall and dark brown with silver-white hair. She had died three years ago in December, and every year, as December got closer, Holly started knitting. She said she didn't even like knitting that much, but it reminded her of her grandmother. By April, the needles would be gone again.

Ashton got quiet.

I don't have to record anybody today, I said. *It's not a big deal.*

I mean, I want to be remembered like everybody else, Ashton said. He kept his eyes on the arm of the desk, tracing circles into it with his thumb and pointer finger. *And I don't want to at the same time.*

I don't get it, Ashton, Amari said, annoyed. He was drawing in his sketchbook. I couldn't see what it was because, as usual, he had his left arm curving over the picture. There was a pack of colored markers by his elbow. *Either you do or you don't.*

Ashton looked right at him. *I don't want to be remembered for saying the wrong thing.*

Ms. Laverne said we can't say anything wrong here, that everything we say is okay and nobody's judging us, Esteban said.

Amari said a curse word. Then looked up with a

cheesy grin. *See? No lightning struck me,* he said, going back to his drawing.

I can't say stuff like how much the gun thing sucks, Ashton said. *But, I mean, does everything have to be about black versus white? I mean, what if people just stopped talking about racism. Wouldn't it just go away? Look at us all sitting here. Everybody is everything and we're all together. And nobody's fighting or being mean to each other.*

Amari stopped drawing and shook his head. *You just don't get it.*

I do too get it, Ashton said. *I didn't even think about being white until the first time I met you, Amari. You asked me if I was an albino. I bet you don't even remember.*

I remember, Amari said.

I didn't even know what an albino was, Ashton said. He pushed his hair away from his forehead.

And that's the problem, Amari said. *Like I said, you just don't get it.*

That's not fair, Amari. I didn't get it, but I knew I didn't like the way it sounded. And I was mad because I thought you guys were laughing at me.

We didn't even know you, Amari said. *Why would we be laughing at you? Why would you think that was . . . that that was what kind of kids we were.*

Because kids are like that, Ashton said.

Not ALL kids. Not us.

The room got so quiet. I think even the hissing of the radiator stopped. Even Holly's needles stopped clicking.

I know you guys aren't like that, Ashton said. He looked at Amari. *You remember what I said back when you asked if I was an albino?*

Yeah. Amari nodded. *You were like, 'No, are you?' And then I said, 'How am I going to be albino and be black like I am?'*

Amari went back to his drawing, but he was smiling a little. *Of course I remember that day,* he said.

I don't know if you remember this part, though.

Amari looked up at him again. *What part?*

You said to me, 'We cool, though, bruh. It's all good. I'm Amari.' And the way your voice sort of just dropped down into something so . . . I don't know, dude. It was so friendly. He pointed to his chest. *I felt myself choking up inside.*

For some reason, when you said that, I missed everything we left in Connecticut a little bit less, you know—our house, our street, my grandma, my school, my friends, all of it. It didn't feel so hard right then, just because you'd said, 'It's all good. I'm Amari.'

Yeah, Amari said. *I remember that. Of course I remember that.*

You do?

Yeah. That's when me and you became friends.

Yeah, Ashton said. *I know.*

They looked at each other. And it was like they had left us. Like they had gone back to that day when they were little kids and were standing in the school yard with the September light shining down on them and kids running all around. The sound of the flag flicking in the wind above them. *It's all good. I'm Amari* were the words raining down over them. Like snow. Like soft and welcoming snow.

21

I've got some more stuff I want to say, Ashton told us. *Haley, I don't care if you record this part.*

I turned the recorder on. Esteban was sitting on the ledge of the window, watching us. Watching all of us. Holly got up and squeezed in beside him. He moved over a bit, making space for her.

Ashton slowly started unwrapping the scarf from around his neck. On one side, we could see finger marks where someone had necked him so hard, they had left the reminder of their own hand. I swallowed.

There are a bunch of kids who aren't very nice here, Ashton said. *The ones that call me Casper and Wonder-bread and Ghostboy and Paleface and other names I don't even want to say.*

Amari looked up and his eyes turned to slits.

Who did that to you?

Ashton shrugged.

Nah, man, tell me. Who did that?

Yeah, Tiago said. *Who did that to you?*

Some eighth-graders, Ashton whispered. *I don't know them. They just do it to be stupid. For laughs.*

You can be stupid and laugh without hitting somebody, Amari said. *That's messed up.*

I know. Ashton gently touched his own neck. *Not like I can do something about it. It's just what happens. Like the way kids laugh at us sometimes in the cafeteria, right? We don't care.*

I care, Holly said. *I know I shouldn't, but I do.*

Me too, Tiago said. *I hate it.*

Yeah, but if we say something, they're just going to laugh harder.

Ashton was right.

We were different, but most days we believed Ms. Laverne when she told us how special we were, how smart, how kind, how beautiful—how tons of successful people had different ways of learning.

But some days, it got inside us. Like now.

||||||||||||||

Where'd they get you, bruh? Amari asked.

Ashton shrugged. *Outside the school yard.*

We all got quiet again.

You know how in the middle of the yard there's that huge flagpole? Ashton said. *And up at the very top there's the flag?*

He looked at each one of us and we all nodded.

Well, on that first day I got here, I stared up at that flag thinking, this is happening all over America. All over America, kids were walking into school yards and classrooms, and the American flag was waving. All over America, kids were saying the Pledge of Allegiance, saying 'indivisible, with liberty and justice for all.' All over America, we had memorized this, but did anybody know what it meant?

Nah, Amari said. *Not really. Not back then.*

I didn't either, Ashton said. *But it gave us a sameness. I stood in the school yard looking up at that flag and I felt something. Not just like a new kid. Not just like a white kid, but like I was a . . . a part of everybody running and jumping and playing all over America. Not just in our school yard. I mean—everywhere.*

I know . . . right? Holly said. *Like, thousands and thousands of kids all over the country got decked out in their new school clothes and were all excited for their first day of school.*

Yeah, Ashton said. *Like that! But on my first day here, almost every kid seemed to be some shade of brown. I had never seen so many brown . . . and black people.* His voice faltered—like he wasn't sure if he was saying it right this time. *So many African . . . Americans.*

And Latinos, Tiago said. *Don't forget us.*

Man, you brown, Amari said. *He already mentioned you.*

Light brown, Holly said. *Light, light, light, light brown.*

I'm not saying anything to be racist, Ashton said. *It's just what I remember. I never even thought about my color till that day. Before I even met you, Amari, it felt like everybody was staring at me.*

Lucky you, Holly said.

How's that lucky?

Because every single body in this room except you had to think about themselves that way already. Like, way before now. The way you felt like you were on the outside of everything? Like you weren't a part of it? Well, that's the way a whole lot of people feel every day.

Amari and Esteban nodded.

It's true, Tiago said. *Like the way people sometimes look at me just because I have an accent, and like Amari with the guns, and like Esteban with his papi—everybody.*

Even me, I said. *The first thing people see is my hair. Then they see my skin.*

Then they ask, 'What are you?' Holly said.

You got the white pass, Ashton. Until now.

I hear you, Ashton said. *But I never asked for a white pass.*

You didn't have to, Holly said. *But all I can say is, welcome home.*

Ashton looked confused until Holly smiled.

You're one of us now.

Ashton leaned back in his chair and, slowly, he smiled. *Yeah,* he said. *I'm one of us now.*

Club Us, Amari said. *The membership requirements are kinda messed up, but whatever.*

I got a question, though, Tiago said. *Why'd your family come all the way here from Connecticut, anyway? The one time my family went to Connecticut, it took us a whole bunch of hours. It was pretty but I'm not trying to be driving for that long. And my mom wouldn't let us play video games. She was like, 'No, we're going to listen to audiobooks.' For hours!*

So not fair! Amari said.

What are you talking about, Holly said. *You like to read, Amari. You read all the time except when you come here. Then you draw. But in class, I always see you with a book.*

Yeah, I know that. You act like that's news.

Then what are you saying?

I didn't say anything about reading. I'm telling the brother it's messed up because you can play a video game and listen to a book. You don't just have to stare out the window. Those are two whole different senses.

That's what's up, Tiago said. *That's what I tried to tell my mom.*

See . . . ?! Amari rolled his eyes at Holly. *Miss Know-It-All think she knows it all.*

But I'm with Tiago, Amari said. *Why'd your peeps come all the way from Connecticut to BK?*

When my dad lost his job in Connecticut, Ashton said, *a friend he knew from college gave him a job managing a Key Food in Brooklyn. I didn't even know what a Key Food was. I guess there are some in Connecticut, but not where we lived.*

Welcome to Brooklyn, Amari said. *We're glad you landed here.*

IIIIIIIIIIIIII

That day, I remember all of us in the ARTT room leaning in toward each other. But what is frozen in my mind, even more than that, is later the same day. Ashton, Amari, Esteban and Tiago left the school together walking four across. So close that their shoulders were touching. Me and Holly walked behind them. A double wall against the neckers who were waiting right outside the school yard. Three tall eighth-graders who glared at Ashton but walked backward, away from the six of us. Three tall eighth-graders who looked from Amari to Tiago to Esteban to Ashton, then kept looking to me and Holly, then turned and walked quickly, really quickly, away from all of us.

22

The first time we saw Esteban smile, really smile again, was in December. It was because of poetry. The Thursday night before, he had gotten a letter from his father, who was still in Florida at the detention center.

At least he's still in this country, Esteban said. *Even though he's far away.*

And he's okay, I said.

Okay-ish, Holly said. *But that's better than nothing, right?*

Esteban had come down from the windowsill and was sitting with us in the circle. He unfolded the letter from his father. It was written on yellow legal pad paper. Esteban handled it delicately as we all leaned in to look at it with him. His father's handwriting was small and careful, each letter so clear, it almost looked typed.

He wrote me a poem, Esteban said. *He said he has time to write now. He said when he writes, it's like he's back in the apartment with us.*

Nobody can touch it, he said.

We all put our hands down in our laps. Even Holly lowered her needles.

That's cool with me, Amari said.

Me too, I said. *But can you read it to us, at least?*

It's in Spanish, Esteban said. *But I wrote an English version too. Because one day, I'm going to be his translator. You guys know what that is, right?*

We nodded, but Esteban was so excited, he explained anyway. *I'm going to rewrite all his poems in English for him. And we're going to sell books in the DR and in America.*

Then Esteban cleared his throat and read.

When they came for me, I lifted my hands to them,
let them wrap the cuffs around my wrists. I did not
fight, I did not yell.
When they pressed me into the van, there were others
who spoke our language—
a language of sun and ocean and beauty, a language
of birds and merengue. We leaned across the van

toward each other and knew the same people back
home.
Always remember, when you are with your people
you are home.

Esteban finished reading the poem and carefully put it back into his notebook. Carefully put his notebook back into his bag.

I kept staring down at my hands, a stone in my throat like I'd choke to death. I saw my father's head again, getting pushed down into the police car. Was he crying when it happened? Did he look toward me? Did he know that everything was gone?

I took a breath. Then another. Air wasn't coming in fast enough.

Haley, I heard Amari say. *You okay, Red?*

I nodded but kept my head down.

It's beautiful, I choked out.

He said he's going to write me more poems, Esteban said. *He said he'll write them until we're all together again.*

He's a good poet, Tiago said. *He reminds me of the other poet guy, the one Ms. Laverne read us. The one who wrote that poem about a blank white page or something.*

Alarcón, Holly said. *Francisco Alarcón.*

I tried to remember Alarcón but couldn't. My head felt so heavy. Maybe this was the weight of the world people talked about. The gray ghost that took your breath and your words.

How do you even remember that? Amari was saying to Holly.

Because she said his name a hundred times AND wrote it on the board. Jeez. How do you not remember that.

Yeah, Tiago said. *That guy.*

He's going to write me more of them, Esteban said. *He promised. And I'll read them in English and Spanish because it's for both languages.*

That's what up, Amari said. *Read those poems in all kinds of American, son.*

When I finally looked up, Esteban was smiling.

23

Outside, the sun is slowly sinking. I hear my uncle drag his suitcase across the floor above me as I listen to Esteban read his father's poem. His voice on the recorder is careful and clear. I wonder if he and his dad are walking along a beach together. I wonder if they're working on their books, Esteban finding the English words for his dad as he writes what he sees. Downstairs, my father has stopped playing piano. Now I hear him moving around in the kitchen, pots being pulled from cabinets, the sound of a bottle of seltzer being opened.

When they came for me, I lifted my hands to them,
let them wrap the cuffs around my wrists. I did not
fight, I did not . . .

Knock knock. My uncle stands at the door, smiling, a bright orange shirt in his hand.

I thought you were going to help me pack, he says. *What about this thing? Stay or go.*

The shirt should go, but you should stay. I turn back to the window, the recorder silent now.

Hales, c'mon, favorite niece.

Only niece.

He comes over to me. Cups my chin and gently turns my head up toward him. His eyes are gray-blue like my father's.

How long has your dad been home?

Two months.

How many conversations have you had with him?

I shrug. *We talk at dinner.*

My uncle shakes his head. *You talk to me at dinner.*

You're like a dad to me, though.

But I'm not him, Haley. I'm not my brother.

I move my head away from his hand, play with the edge of my comforter.

All the questions I could never answer, Haley. That's your guy—right downstairs. He's as afraid of you as you are of him.

I don't say anything.

Cousins.

What? I look up at him.

Don't you want some cousins to boss around? Some bigheaded boy cousins or some cutie-cute baby girl cousins.

What are you talking about?

The sooner I get out of here, the sooner the ladies will come running. The sooner I'll find someone and get busy making you some cousins.

Ugh. That's gross, I say. But I'm laughing. *You're so gross and that's so TMI.*

He holds up the shirt again, looks at it a second, then tosses it on my head. *Keep it,* he says. *I bet it'll look good on you.*

By the time I get it off my head, he's gone back upstairs.

I close my door, then turn the recorder back on, fast-forwarding. Past Holly and Tiago and more Amari. And then it is me, telling my story for the first time. While my uncle packs. While my dad plays piano. My own voice in the ARTT room then, but in my room now . . . *The thing I've never told you guys is that my dad's in prison.*

24

My uncle and I had been in the car for more than an hour and were finally out of the city. The tall buildings had shrunk down into trees and long ribbons of wild, dying grass. The sun wasn't up yet and everything looked like it had been painted in black and dark blue.

Years had passed since that afternoon on the slide. A tiny scar shaped like a *Z* ran from my hairline down behind my right ear. I reached up and ran my finger along it. My uncle used to say being a parent meant long nights and short years. He said before anyone blinked, kids were grown up, packing their bags and moving on. But some things stayed. The scar. The memory of that day on the slide. My mother's nails. My voice on the recorder. Esteban's hug.

I must have slept because when I looked out the window again, we were passing the New Paltz exit and the sun was beginning to rise over the mountains. The sky was burgundy and blue. I've only seen the sky this way driving to Malone. It seemed strange that there could be so much color and beauty, and then when you got to Malone everything was tan and gray and black steel bars and wire.

You know they found Esteban's dad in Florida, I said, staring out the window.

Who?

Esteban. The guy from my class! My friend. They took his dad. Esteban!

My uncle glanced at me and nodded. *Oh right. I know who Esteban is,* he said. *But I didn't know his dad was gone.*

But I thought— And then I remembered. Of course I hadn't told him. We didn't talk to anyone outside the ARTT room about the things we talked about inside it. We talked and talked and talked but only to each other. The day before, Ms. Laverne had found the six of us sitting in the corner of the lunchroom, laughing at a character Tiago was mimicking. Even Esteban had thrown his head back and cracked up. We were all huddled into one another, shoulders pressing against shoulders, Holly's legs thrown over mine.

Immigration took his dad, I told my uncle slowly.

Oh jeez, Haley. I had no idea. I'm so sorry. I can't believe this crap is happening right in Brooklyn.

I looked at him and said, *Brooklyn's part of America.* I felt tired. Was Esteban awake? Had he gotten another poem? Did they know anything else about what was happening? On Friday he'd looked like he hadn't slept. He'd kept his head down in class most of the day. I didn't know how to tell my uncle all of this without getting so sad and feeling like a dumb kid who couldn't even help her friend.

Hales, I'm so sorry, he said again. *What next for them? What's the plan? Should I reach out to his mother?*

His mom is hoping some lawyers can do something. But he said she's packing. Packing and waiting.

I didn't want to talk about it anymore. It suddenly felt like I was betraying Esteban, betraying the ARTT room. My uncle was a grown-up. What did he understand about six kids talking? What did anybody besides me, Tiago, Holly, Amari, Esteban and Ashton understand? Nothing. Nothing at all.

Jeez, my uncle said again.

Yeah, I said. *Jeez.*

Outside, the farther we got into the mountains, the faster the wind rushed past the car. I leaned against the window. My uncle drove in silence. The mountains went from burgundy to pink to green and brown. The sun, as always, rose.

25

This time, when we got to Malone, my dad came down immediately and hugged me so hard, I thought my shoulder bones would crack. He and my uncle looked so much alike, no one could ever say they weren't brothers, but now my dad looked so much older. He had dark circles under his eyes and was wearing the glasses with thick black frames that he usually only put on to read.

I just couldn't get myself down here last time, my dad said. *I'm so sorry. I was having one of those days and it turned into the longest month of my life.*

I stood there listening to him. I wanted to tell him that when someone drives almost to Canada to see you, you ignore those days. You push past them. I wanted to ask him how come I knew this as a kid and he didn't know it as a grown-up?

But I didn't say any of this. I just nodded, said, *It's okay. At least we're all together now, right?* Because that part was true. I thought about Esteban's father being so far away from him and him not even able to visit.

I looked over at my uncle. He was standing with his hands in his pockets, his feet a little bit apart. He and my father both looked so worried and sad.

I nodded and said, *I get it, Dad,* because what if next time he didn't come down again? Or what if the car accident had taken both of my parents from me and he wasn't even here for me to be mad at? What if my uncle had been in the back seat?

My dad hugged me again. His prison uniform felt the same—stiff against my cheek, familiar as daylight. I had never seen him in anything but those tan khaki pants and a tan shirt with a number on the pocket. After all those years, I should've known that number by heart. There was so much I wanted to remember, so many stories. But his number wasn't one of them. The story of his number was one I'd lock away in a room and write on the door of that memory *The End*.

26

As we drove home that afternoon, I pulled my braids down over my eyes and thought about Kira's hands in my hair, the way they felt strong and warm and sure—the tiny point of her comb making straight parts between the braids, the smell of the lavender oil she rubbed into my scalp. I had sat there the way I did every time she did my hair—with my eyes closed and my head tilted down—secretly imagining Kira was my mother. I know that's stupid. Holly was sitting across from us, talking away and eating pretzels with peanut butter. I imagined my mom had put the bowl where it was between us. I imagined she'd said, *You've always loved pretzels and peanut butter, Haley. I remember when you were a baby, you grabbed a spoon full of peanut butter out of my hand*

and shoved it into your mouth. I was so scared. All those stories I'd heard about peanut butter allergies and how babies shouldn't have it until they were older. I tried to pry your mouth open with my fingers and scoop it out . . .

But it was Kira talking, Kira who had pried Holly's mouth open. Kira's fear.

I let out a deep breath and felt my uncle glance over at me.

Tell me about her again, I said. *The little bit you know.*

About your mom, right? my uncle said. *I figured that's where you had gone.*

I nodded.

I only knew her a short time, he said. *By the time Berry and your dad got really serious, I was already away at college. I hardly ever came home. You know our dad didn't approve, right?*

Yeah, I said. *But he died before I was born, and you and Dad used some of the money he left you to buy our house. Too bad so sad for him, I guess.*

Are you mocking me?

I shook my head. *Nope, just saying what you always say. Your dad wasn't a nice guy. But at least you got to know your mom, even though you were young when she died. I wish I had known mine.*

You would have loved her like crazy, Hales, my uncle said. *And she would have been over the moon about you. She* was *over the moon about you.*

How many times had he started the story this same way? I knew exactly what he'd say next, and in my head, I said it with him. *Your parents loved each other like that romantic movie kind of love. Except it was real. They truly, truly loved each other.*

My mother and father had met when they were both at Brooklyn College. My mother was studying to be a nurse and my father wanted to be a teacher. They had some kind of advanced science class together. My uncle was still in high school then. He said my dad told him he'd never even imagined the two of them falling in love. It didn't even feel like a possibility.

But then it happened, my uncle said. *And your dad, when he told me about her, he just said, 'She's the most amazing person I've ever met. You're gonna love her.' He didn't say 'She's the most amazing black person I've ever met.' So I was surprised when I first met her.*

That's racist, I said.

Nah, it's just truth. I was a young knucklehead with a skinny brain. And then I wasn't anymore.

She changed you, I said. *She woke you up.*

Both of you woke me up. And keep on waking me up. He tapped my head.

The sun was starting to set and the sky was a bright orange now. Upstate was so different from Brooklyn. There weren't buildings blocking the sky, and the mountains felt like they were just there to let color slip through them and around them. Just there to help us see it all.

Your mother would always try to pinch my cheek when I first met her, my uncle was saying. *'You're such a cutie,' she'd say every time she saw me! Man, I'd get so mad about it. I mean, it wasn't like I was some little kid like you—*

Hey!

You know what I mean. I was fifteen! Fifteen is almost a man.

Almost, Uncle. Just almost. But not.

She was only five years older than me. I always loved to see her smiling. And it was so easy to make her laugh. He glanced at me.

When you smile, it reminds me of her.

I smiled into the window, trying to imagine my twenty-year-old not-yet-mother pinching my uncle's cheek. I could see her hands, dark with the bright red polish. But her face and hair were blurred.

She was tall, I said.

Taller than your dad.

And someone in her family had red hair too, I said. *But not her.*

Red hair on both sides, my uncle said. *You were doomed.*

I was doomed.

My uncle laughed. Behind his glasses, I could see the lines at the edges of his eyes. Crow's-feet. That's what he said people called them. *Tiny maps of my life,* he'd say.

They were beautiful.

We drove for a while without talking. We were listening to Joni Mitchell—a singer from way back before my uncle was a kid. She was singing about the color green. She had another song about the color blue, but the green song was one of my favorites. Her voice was sweet and high but she could make it do crazy things and hold notes for so long, like, it made your eyes water. My uncle sang along with her. *There'll be icicles and birthday clothes and sometimes there'll be sorrow.*

The story is not complicated. Since that time in the hospital, I'd asked my uncle about it again and again. I was born when my parents were both twenty-six. Then when I was three, they got into a car accident coming back from a party. My dad was driving, and when they got a block away from home, my dad accidentally hit the accelerator instead of the brake and mowed into a lamppost before swerving the car and hitting the outside wall of a donut shop. It was nearly morning and the streets were empty, so nobody came when he screamed for help. So he stumbled home to get my uncle to help him get my mom out of the car. *She won't move,* he kept saying. *She won't wake up!* My uncle's voice gets quiet when he tells that part of the story. My dad's nose was broken and he had cuts on his hands and arms. My uncle was babysitting me. Before the three of us could get back to the car, the cops pulled up beside us and arrested my dad for leaving the scene of a crime. And for drunk driving.

He kept saying to me, my uncle told me, *'Go get her. Please go make her wake up.'*

My mother was six days away from her thirtieth birthday. But by the time the cops booked my father, my mother had been dead for hours. She will always be twenty-nine.

Sometimes I say the words slowly to myself. *Vehicular homicide.* It sounds like a hiccup. Or like the first words of a song. It sounds like the promise of something. And then it doesn't.

Tell me again about the day after the accident, I said.

I told you your mom and dad both had to go away, my uncle said. *I told you I'd keep you safe, though. That you didn't have to worry. And that you'd see your daddy again soon. I told you I loved you and that I'd always take care of you.*

And I asked you who would take care of me all day, and you said, 'We're good, Red. I can do it.'

That I did.

That's what you used to call me. Before I made you stop.

Yup.

And I said, 'Does that mean I'm white now?'

My uncle smiled. *You sure did. And I said nope.*

You said I'd always be half white and half black.

And that until it turned gray, you'd always have red hair.

Tell me again how I made you stop calling me Red.

You said, 'My name is Haley, not Red!' And not quietly either. My uncle laughed. *I'd never heard you have so much conviction before that day.*

I thought about Amari calling me Red and how I didn't mind it so much when he said it.

And what did you think about how I said it?

I thought, I'm raising a strong brave girl. I'm doing something right.

I leaned across the car and rested my head against his arm. *Sometimes I don't feel so brave. Sometimes I just feel scared.*

I know, he said. *That makes two of us.*

27

You think he's coming back? Ashton asked. *I don't know his phone number or anything.*

It was Thursday and Esteban had been absent the whole week. The five of us sat in the corner of the cafeteria, not touching our food, while rain slammed against the windows.

Ms. Laverne said she's trying to find out what's happening, Holly said. *But the number the school has for him is disconnected.*

Yeah, Amari said. *Esteban doesn't have his own phone. Remember I used to let him play games on mine?* Amari stopped talking and shook his head. *I mean, not* I used to. *He always plays games on mine. That's what I meant to say. And when he gets back to school, I'm gonna keep letting him do it.*

But—, I started to say.

No buts, *Red. You have to think positive.*

I don't think he would move away without saying goodbye to us, Ashton said. *We're his friends.*

But they take people, Tiago said. *In the night. In the morning. They just take them. Like they took his dad. So what if they came in the night and took E and his family.*

But they can't, Ashton said. *Esteban and his sister, both of them were born here.*

I know . . . right? Amari said. He looked around the cafeteria. It was loud with the sound of trays banging and kids yelling. Someone blew a whistle and for a moment everything went silent. But then a boy at the far end of the cafeteria held up the whistle he had blown and it was like someone turned on the sound again. I watched a teacher go over to him and take the whistle away.

His dad wrote good poetry, Holly said.

Writes, I said. *He* writes *good poetry. They're not dead, guys.*

It just sucks, Amari said. *Here we are, trying to have the ARTT room, and boom, it gets messed up like this. I mean, Esteban, he's cool. He's nice. He makes us . . . the six of us. It's not fair.*

Nah, it's not, Holly said. *This is supposed to be America. The land of the free and the home of the brave.*

Amari was drinking milk and he laughed so hard, it came spraying out of his mouth and nose all over the table and Holly.

So gross! Holly said. *Oh my God! You are so, so gross!* She wiped her shirt and hands with a tissue. Milk sprinkled her sandwich, so she pushed her whole tray away.

My bad, Amari said, but he was still laughing.

Then he stopped and looked at us all. *I got one word for you,* Amari said. *Lenape.*

What about them?

You think they were somewhere saying, 'Well, this is supposed to be the land of the free and the home of the brave'? Nah, man. They were here in Lenapehoking, aka New York City, getting robbed. They were getting gangstered by the so-called settlers. You miss that whole history lesson?

Holly glared at him. *No, I didn't miss that whole history lesson,* she said, mocking him.

Then how you going to be trying to erase them? You're doing the same thing the people who took E's dad are doing. Up here trying to erase people.

No I'm not! Holly yelled. We got quiet. Amari looked around the cafeteria. People were staring at us. One of the eighth-graders who had necked Ashton gave us the finger, and Tiago, Amari and Ashton jumped out of their seats and lurched toward him. But the boy put up his hands in an all's-cool way and they sat back down. Ashton's neck was back to its pale skinny self. There was something both heartbreaking and awesome about that big boy being scared of some fifth/sixth grade *special* kids.

C'mon, guys, Tiago said. *E will be back. We don't need to be fighting about it. He wouldn't want that.*

Nah, we all agreed. *He wouldn't.*

28

On Friday, Esteban was still gone.

Amari came into the ARTT room saying, *The great imperfect world continues to spin on a slant.* He threw his hands up like he'd just said something amazing. We just looked at him, waiting for him to say something else. But he didn't. He took his seat, looked over at Esteban's empty spot by the window and took out his markers.

Tiago reached for the recorder.

We all froze. Even Amari, his drawing pad halfway out of his backpack, the colored markers gathered in their rubber band on his desk.

Maybe for a millisecond, the world stopped spinning. Maybe Esteban, wherever he was, turned toward the ARTT room and smiled.

Can I record myself today? Tiago asked.

The four of us nodded, our mouths slightly open.

He pressed the record button, cracked his left knuckles with his right hand. And started talking.

So now it's almost wintertime, right. And we've been coming here for so long, I feel like I know you guys and you're sort of like my brothers and sisters and I know I can trust you, right?

We all nodded.

I feel like there's love in this room. I know that sounds corny, but I feel it. He hit his chest. *Right here I feel like we care about each other. Even Esteban.* Tiago kissed his pointer and middle finger and raised them into the air. *Wherever he is, he's our brother and he's our friend and a part of him is in this room.*

We kissed our own fingers and raised them into the air, nodding.

I want tell you the story of Perrito. He was my dog. He was part Doberman, part Labrador. He was the best dog. He was my best friend. He spoke Spanish and English. Sometimes, when Ms. Laverne asks us to write in class, it's hard for me. The words don't want to come. I see you guys all writing and writing and I want to do that too. But the words I write want to come out in Spanish, not English. And people are always saying, 'Speak English! Speak English!' Not you guys! When you see me and

Esteban talking in Spanish, you just say, 'Teach me.' You don't say mean things. Once when me and my mom were walking down the block speaking in Spanish, this guy yelled at us, 'This is America! Speak English!' But I'm from Puerto Rico, and Puerto Rico is part of the United States of America too, so Spanish should be American, right?

We all agreed. Amari was drawing but he kept nodding with the rest of us. Tiago's quiet was beginning to make sense to us.

But me and my mom didn't say anything, Tiago said. *Because that guy was big and he looked mad. If Perrito had been with us, I bet that guy wouldn't have said anything. Perrito was big too. And the Doberman part of him was mad protective of us. When me and my mom got to the next block, we started talking again, but my mom was whispering and I was sad that that guy with his red angry face made my mom quieter.*

The four of you guys—he pointed to me, Ashton, Holly and Amari—*you guys* only *speak English, and I'm not saying there's something wrong with that*—

But, dude, Amari said, *Puerto Rico's a part of this country and you speak English too.*

Yeah, I know, Tiago said. *But I only speak in Spanish with my family. And in PR, even though we had to speak*

English and Spanish in school, I still liked speaking in Spanish better. His voice dropped and he looked down at his hands. *And because I came from Puerto Rico, I'm safe. I don't have to worry. Not for myself and my family. Just for my friends.*

He stared at the voice recorder for a long time.

My mom, when she's at home, she loves to sing in Spanish. She talks in Spanish. She cooks in Spanish. It feels like she even laughs in Spanish, because her smile gets so, so big. But when she goes outside now, she is very quiet, because she's afraid another person like that guy will look inside her mouth and see Puerto Rico there. Not the beach or the sparkling blue ocean. Not the awesome pastelillos or the quenepas that are so sweet, you can't stop eating them. She thinks they'll see her small town of Isabela, where her dad raised chickens and on holidays her abuela made arroz the old way, on a fire outside, and everybody begged for the pegao—the crispy rice that stuck to the bottom of the pot. She thinks people here will say, 'Go back to your country.' Even though this is her country.

And it hurts her. It makes her sad and ashamed. Because if somebody keeps saying and saying something to you, you start believing it, you know. My mom has the past dreams of Puerto Rico and the future dream of this place. And this place acts like it doesn't have any future dreams of us.

In English, Perrito means 'Little Dog.' Our dog was just a tiny black puppy when we got him. He could almost fit in my hand, he was so small. Some people couldn't say his name right because you have to kind of roll your tongue to say the sound of the two r's *together. Not everybody can do that.*

We all tried to do it—to say *Perrito* like Tiago did. Only Amari could say it right, though.

I wanted to give him a name not everybody could say, Tiago told us. *I wanted to make him even more special than he already was. I could whisper it and he would come running. His hearing was crazy good. When people called his name in English—without doing the right thing with the* r's*—he wouldn't even lift his head. When he was dying last year, I put his head in my lap and I just kept petting him. I said his name real soft, over and over and over. 'Perrito. Perrito. Perrito.' I wasn't scared. He just kept looking more and more peaceful. And then his breath kept getting faster and faster like maybe in his mind he was somewhere winning a race. And then his breathing stopped. And his eyes closed. I put my face against his head and I said, 'You won, Perrito. You won* *the race.' And my mom let me stay like that for a long time. Just me and Perrito's body and the quiet.*

Tiago stopped talking. He had tears in his eyes, but he wasn't crying. Not really. Then the tears were spilling over. We didn't look at him. It felt like it would be wrong to stare or say anything. He was in his own world. He was back with Perrito, his face on Perrito. Ahead of them both—the finish line.

I know in my heart, Tiago whispered, *the language we like to speak is music and poetry and even cold, sweet piraguas on hot, hot summer days. But it feels like this place wants to break my heart. It feels like every day it tries to make my mom feel tinier and tinier, like the size of Perrito's head in my hands.*

29

The next week, just as we were getting ready to do math problems, Esteban walked back into our classroom. Ms. Laverne didn't even try to keep us from jumping out of our seats to hug him and slap his back and say *Where were you?* and *We were so scared you had left forever* and *Is your dad home?*

He's still gone, in Florida, Esteban said when we'd finally calmed down. *But he sent me another poem.* Amari had his arm over Esteban's shoulder and Tiago was standing as close to him as could be. The rest of us had gone back to our seats, but we were all staring at E in wonder. It felt magical to have him back. It felt like we were almost perfect again.

Ms. Laverne asked him to come up to the front of the class to read the poem to us, and when Amari finally let go of him, he carefully removed a piece of yellow paper from between his notebook pages. His uniform was clean but wrinkled, and the dark circles under his eyes looked like they covered most of his face now. He looked skinnier too.

We moved to live with my aunt in Queens, he said. *And one of my crazy baby cousins tried to eat this.* He held up the poem. The edge had a tiny bite taken out of it. Esteban shook his head, but he was smiling.

I'm going to read it in Spanish first, Esteban said. He read, and even though I didn't understand the words, they were so beautiful they sounded like music, and I put my head down on my desk to listen better.

Now I'm going to read the English translation that I made for you. He looked at the five of us, then at Ms. Laverne. He seemed older somehow. Like he had gone away and lived a whole life and then came back to us.

And in the night, when the dog barks at shadows,
tell him
not to be afraid of what he cannot see
or the things he does not yet understand.
There is mystery everywhere.
Beneath rocks, there is damp earth
and an army of ants
planning a revolution.

Esteban stood at the front of the room, staring at the page. Then he lifted his head and looked at us. We cheered again, even louder this time. I don't know if any of us really understood his dad's poem. But for a long time after he'd finished reading, I thought about that army of ants, how they were coming together.

Like us.

30

And in the night, when the dog barks at shadows, tell him / not to be afraid . . .

In the cafeteria that day, Esteban asked if he could record the poems he had read to us. *I don't know if I'm going to be here tomorrow,* he said. *Or the next day or the day after that.*

But I thought you were back, son, Amari said.

Esteban looked down at his empty tray. He had eaten everything on it so fast, Amari handed over his milk and I gave him my leftover beef taco.

We don't know what's going to happen, he told us later when we got to the ARTT room. *They might be trying to deport my mami too, and that's why we moved to my aunt's house. It's like my mami has to hide now.*

But why? Ashton asked.

Esteban shrugged. *She's from the DR too. My aunt, she was born here, and her husband is from America. My mami said if she gets sent back, me and my sister can stay with my aunt, but I don't want that.*

He climbed up to his place by the window, but he didn't get quiet and stare out. He turned toward us and crossed his legs. When he did, I saw the holes in the bottoms of his shoes. His socks, which were probably bright white when they were new, were grayish and barely covered his ankles. His uniform pants were too short now.

I turned on the recorder and put it on my desk. Esteban nodded, repeated what he had just said and continued.

They took my papi. They came to his job when he was leaving and they said he didn't belong in this country. Maybe always in his heart he knew the day was coming. When I was little, he used to always say to me, 'Every day is a blessing from God, Esteban. Even if it rains or gets so cold you can see your breath and think your own bones are going break beneath your skin—this too is God's blessing.' My papi said, 'One day, your days are all gone. And then—that's when you have nothing.'

I was probably a stupid little kid whining because I wanted a toy or ice cream. I don't even remember. But now I know something. I know we had everything we needed. We had food every day. And coats. And boots and warm socks. And water.

Before, you used to hear the word immigration *and it sounded like everything you ever believed in. It sounded like* feliz cumpleaños *and* merry Christmas *and* welcome home. *But now you hear it and you get scared because it sounds like a word that makes you want to disappear. It sounds like someone getting stolen away from you.*

What's gonna happen, E? Amari asked.

Esteban shrugged. *My mami says you have to pay for lawyers and stuff to fight it, but we don't have money for that. I think . . . I think we're all going to have to go back to the DR. And that would suck, because I would miss New York and I would miss all of you guys.*

We sat there, silent, all of us looking at Esteban. It felt like he was already almost gone. And we were trying hard to remember him.

31

After Christmas vacation, everyone returned looking a little bit different. But the thing that mattered the most was that Esteban had come back too. Tiago came back wearing glasses, thin wire frames that he took off to show us how they caught the light and bounced rainbows around the room. They reminded me of my uncle's glasses. I watched Tiago place them gently back over his nose. Years from now, I thought, there'll be people who never knew Tiago before glasses.

Those are nice kicks, Ashton said, staring longingly at Holly's sneakers. *Those are the ones I asked for for Christmas. But I got these instead.* Ashton made a face and held up his feet. His sneakers were white and cheap-looking, like the kind they sold in discount stores. *And my mom started singing that 'you get what you get' song when I complained.* He put his feet down. *You lucked out, Hols.*

It's not luck, Amari said. *Holly's a rich girl. Everybody knows that.*

No I'm not, Holly said. *Don't start in on me, Amari.* But Holly pulled her feet back like she was embarrassed by her sneakers.

I had gone with her and Kira the day she got them. Her mom took one look at the price and called on Jesus. Nobody in their house is religious, but for some reason, that's what came to her lips when she saw the price.

But I love them! Holly said. *And they can be one of my Christmas presents. And plus, those are what everybody's wearing.*

I waited for Kira to say what she always said to Holly—*If everybody jumped off a bridge . . .* But she didn't. *I'm going to get you these,* she said really soft so that Holly had to stop tying the sneakers and look up to hear her. *But I want you to know that everybody is* not *wearing them. I want you to understand what that means.*

Holly nodded. A look came over her—as though the words were finding a room in her brain. *Jeez, Ma. I know,* she said.

Sometimes I thought Kira didn't know Holly like I knew her. Some days I saw her looking at her daughter like she couldn't believe they were related. But it wasn't Holly's fault that she had always known she could walk into a store and ask for expensive sneakers and get them. And Holly was really generous. Even when we were little, she made sure I had whatever she had—from candy to new comic books to time with Kira. She made her mom buy two of things and always had one waiting for me. *I don't want to have this alone,* she would say. *That's not even a little bit fun.*

Wish I had such nice kicks, rich girl, Amari whispered loud enough for everyone to hear. He was not going to drop it.

Delete you, Amari, Holly blurted out. *Why are you even in my ear?*

You two just love to argue, I said. *My uncle says that sometimes two people come into the world having the same fight they left the world having.*

Holly looked at me. *What does that even mean?*

I pointed to her and Amari. *You two. Maybe in another life you guys were having this fight. My uncle says people just keep getting reincarnated into each other's lives until they figure it out.*

Tiago laughed. *You guys been fighting since the days of dinosaurs.*

I don't know. No offense, Amari, Holly said, *but you better not be getting all up in my next life. I don't even like you in this one.*

What's not to like about Amari? Ashton said. *There's Not Really anything not to like about him.*

Yeah, Tiago said. *He's Not Really. I mean he's not really a bad guy. Not Really.*

The boys laughed. Even Esteban, who was sitting in the window seat watching the sleet come down. He had draped his Yankees jacket over his shoulders like a cape.

Amari smiled. *I shouldn't have ever told y'all about that name,* he said.

But Amari wasn't really laughing with his friends. He was studying Holly. It dawned on me then, clear and loud as a siren, that it mattered to Amari what Holly thought about him. Her words had stung. And just like our tilting earth, Amari was off balance, hurt by her words.

I touched Holly's arm. Couldn't she see it? The way Amari's face had dropped?

You don't really not like him, right, Holly? I tried to get her to look at me, to see me pleading with her.

She shrugged. The room got eerily quiet. Before I could say anything else, Holly said, *Nobody chooses where they get born or who they get born to. Maybe my parents are rich, but that doesn't mean I am. I mean, I am now, I guess, but . . .* Holly looked up at Amari. *It's not my fault.*

I don't think Ms. Laverne wanted us to not like each other in this room, Tiago said. *I think she wanted us to get closer. Not more far away from each other.*

Holly picked up her knitting needles. She knitted slowly now, like her mind was someplace else. Her feet were still tucked beneath her chair. *If anybody in this room wanted these sneakers, I'd give them to you.*

My uncle says our lives are dashes—from birth to death. And each day is a new dash, another day, another chance. I wanted to tell him that people are dashes too—each a tiny bit of a connection to the next.

Holly glanced over at Amari, then down at his drawing and back at him again.

I don't like when you call me rich girl, Mar, she said.

Amari shrugged. *Then I won't anymore. That's all you had to say. You didn't have to come at me all mean and whatnot.*

Dash to dash, my uncle would say. Holly to Amari. Me to Holly. Perrito to Tiago. Esteban to his father. Amari to Ashton. Ms. Laverne to all of us. My uncle said when people come together and they all care about the same things, it's called a Harmonic Convergence. He said all that energy together can shift a whole planet.

The sleeting stopped. The sun came out.

We good? Amari asked.

And Holly said, *Yeah, Amari. We're good.*

32

How come you haven't talked about your dad in the ARTT room? Holly asked me.

It was Friday night and almost nine thirty. My hair was washed, oiled and cornrowed. Kira had finished it while me and Holly ate spinach pizza at the kitchen table. Now Kira had gone off to a movie with Holly's father, and the babysitter was downstairs asleep on the couch. How many Fridays had I spent in this house? In this room? So many, I had lost count. If someone spun me around a hundred times and drove me all over Brooklyn, then walked me blindfolded back into Holly's house, I would know it. I would know the smell of it—oil soap and fireplace wood. I would know the sound of it—a creaking fifth step between the second and third floors, creaking banister between the first and second. And if Kira held out her hand to me, I would know it was hers by the softness of her fingers, the length of her nails, the many, many times I'd felt its weight on my head.

We were sitting on Holly's queen-size bed, combing her dolls' hair. Holly had white everything on her bed—sheets, comforter, pillowcases—because she had insisted on dark purple walls. Kira wouldn't say yes unless everything else in the room was white. On the floor beside the bed was a round white shag rug. The doll I had was wearing a green nightgown. Holly's doll was in overalls, and we had changed their outfits twice already. The dolls all had stories and books that came with them about how they had gotten to be true Americans. They were expensive, and while Holly had all of them, I only had one, a doll who had escaped slavery and gotten free in Philadelphia. We could go months without even looking at the dolls, then other times we played with them for hours.

You haven't told them about your dad—or your mom, Holly said. *Are you going to?* She stopped braiding her doll's hair and looked at me.

But I do talk, I said. *I talk into the recorder at night. In my room. I'm on there too.*

I don't know . . . , Holly said. *I don't know if that's fair for everybody. Everybody else is spilling their guts and you're talking in private. Are you ashamed of your life?*

No! Of course not.

But Holly kept looking at me. She blinked slowly.

I don't have anything to be ashamed of, I said.

Then how come you don't talk about your dad. Or tell them about your uncle. All the times Amari's called me 'rich girl,' you just sat there.

What did you want me to say?

Holly shrugged.

No, Holly. Tell me. What did you want me to say?

I wanted you to say, 'I'm a rich girl too!'

But I'm not.

Holly shook her head.

I'm not. I felt my voice getting high.

Haley, listen to me. Your uncle owns that whole building you live in. He drives a nice car. He works at home doing tech stuff when he wants. But he doesn't have *to. Not like my dad. Not like Amari's dad or all the other kids' parents either. When your grandparents died, they left your uncle and dad all their money. When your mom died, they put all the insurance money in the bank for you. When you turn twenty-one, you get it.*

How do you even know this? I said. I mean, I knew

some of it—like about the building and stuff—but I never thought of us as rich.

Your uncle and my mom talk, that's how. Grown-ups tell each other things and then they talk to other grown-ups, and sometimes us kids are around listening.

I didn't say anything. It felt strange. Weird. Rich? My uncle never bought me expensive clothes. We never went on fancy vacations, and most of our furniture was stuff my uncle had bought from thrift shops. He found the coffee table on the street. One leg was shorter than the other three.

Holly put her doll on the pillow and leaned against the wall behind the bed.

I'm not trying to be mean to you, Haley. I know sometimes it sounds that way because I just . . . say stuff.

I know you're not being mean, I said, but I kept my eyes on the doll. Her tiny earrings sparkled.

I think sometimes, Holly said slowly, as though the idea was just now coming to her, *life gives you stuff you don't want, but you have to take it anyway.*

Like my hair, I said. *Or what happened with my mom and dad.*

Holly nodded. *Yeah. But your hair is amazing.*

And all the stuff you know is amazing, Holly. After a minute, after thinking about what she said about me being rich, after knowing that she was right and that maybe somewhere, buried with a lot of other stuff, I knew it too, I said, *And you make us think.*

Holly shrugged, then grabbed up a bunch of her braids with both hands. *But sometimes my mouth hurts people too. Like, I hate that I can't stop it from saying things—and can't stop my body from jumping up and moving around when Ms. Laverne tells us to stay in our seats. Sometimes I just want to be regular . . .*

But you're not regular. You're Holly. I love your big mouth and your jumpy body. And how you make us all laugh—in a good way!

Holly got up from the bed and started walking fast, back and forth, across the room.

I used to think ARTT started mostly because of me and you, she said. *I know that's crazy. I mean, think about it.* She stopped pacing and looked at me. *If I hadn't met you, it wouldn't be the six of us. We're lucky the way we all got dropped there, the way we all ended up in Ms. Laverne's class together, right? All of that happened because* a, b *and* c *happened, and that led to* d, e *and* f *and so on, until basically your life is the whole alphabet. And the alphabet is people meeting people, leading to other people meeting, until we're old. And then we die.*

Or sometimes we're not old and we die, I said quietly.

Yeah . . . Holly climbed on the bed and put her arms around me. *That's true too.*

I'll talk, I said. *Next Friday.*

And I'll be there right next to you, okay?

That night, as always, we slept with our backs to each other, our spines, as always, touching.

33

The following Friday, Holly sat next to me and nodded toward the recorder. My own hands were sweating as I pressed the button and looked up at the others. I was surprised how nervous I was. No one had ever said "don't talk about your dad," but for some reason I had buried the story deep, and now I was going to tell it. To my friends. I kept saying that again and again in my head. They're your friends, Haley. They're your friends.

But just as I turned on the recorder, Esteban said, *I have another poem from my papi,* and Amari said, *Yes!* Holly nodded at me. Esteban climbed down from the window seat and pulled the poem from his pocket. It was as wrinkled as his uniform.

I have to keep it on me, he said. *Crazy baby cousin always takes my things and messes with them. I put the other poems up on a shelf, but he can climb.* Esteban smiled and shook his head. He looked tired but happy as he unfolded the poem, holding the page at its edges. His hands trembled as he read first the Spanish and then, more slowly and beautifully, the English.

And when darkness came and the night
felt like it wanted to swallow me
the echo of 'Lights out!' was thrown
back at the guards in so many beautiful languages
that it sounded like the song the world
has been trying to teach us
since the beginning of time.

He folded the poem carefully and put it back in his pocket. *It means that there are all these different kinds of people in detention with my papi. And when the guards tell them that it's time for lights-out, they all yell it back in their own language, so my papi hears all the languages and it's like they're singing him to sleep.* Esteban touched the pocket with the poem in it. *That's all I have to say for now.* He climbed back onto the window ledge and wrapped his arms around his legs, resting his head on his knees.

After everyone told him how beautiful the poem was, I stood up.

I want to talk now, I said. *You guys have all told your stories about your families, and there's a story I haven't told you.* I looked over at Holly and she nodded again. *It's about my . . . life. It's about my father.* Esteban turned to me. *And my mother,* I said, my voice cracking. *It's about what happened to me when I was little and when I first met Holly's mom, Kira . . .*

34

The first time I met Holly's mom, I was seven years old, and Holly and I had only known each other for a few months. Kira, Holly's mom, had asked my uncle about doing my hair and he agreed. No, he hadn't agreed—he nearly jumped into her arms before she could even get the words out.

So the first time I was at their house, when I was sitting in their kitchen with my hair washed and dripping onto the towel, and Kira asked about my full name, about my family . . .

The rest of the group got so quiet, I stopped talking. My throat felt like it was closing up.

You got this, Red, Amari said to me. His smile loosened the words.

I looked at Holly helplessly. *It's okay,* she said. *I'm here with you. I can help if you need me.*

Everyone nodded. I smiled at her, relieved, and Holly put her arm around me.

The thing I've never told you guys is that my dad's in prison.

Your dad's in prison?! Tiago and Amari said at the same time.

I nodded.

For what? Tiago asked. *Did he rob somebody?*

He was driving, I said slowly. *He was driving a car. My mother was in it.*

The room felt like it was breathing for me. As I told the story of the accident, Esteban's eyes filled and Ashton put his head down on his hands. When I got to the part about my father running home for my uncle's help, Amari said, *Jeez, Red, I didn't even know.* He said it quietly, almost under his breath, but in the words there was so much love that it felt like he was reaching across the circle and hugging me.

Holly was holding on to my hand now.

Is he in jail for life? Amari asked finally. *And plus, I'm sorry about your mom.*

He's going to be coming out soon, I said. *I'm not exactly sure when.*

This is too deep, Amari said. *No wonder you so quiet, Red. You all kinds of still water.*

When I first met Kira, she asked me about my people, and I told her my mom died. I waited for her to say something like 'I'm so sorry' or 'you poor baby' or 'oh sweetie' . . . but she didn't. She was combing my hair at the time, and she stopped for a minute and her hand got real shaky.

I remember you told my mom that your mom died when you were three, Holly said. *And that you didn't really remember her.*

My mami's still with us, Esteban said. *I feel lucky for that.*

But why was her hand shaky? Ashton asked. *Was she feeling sad for you?*

No! Holly said. *That's the crazy part.* She jumped up from her seat, then sat down again real fast and started tapping her feet like I wasn't telling the story fast enough. *Tell them, Haley!*

I'm trying! I said. *Kira asked me if I was Beryl Anderson's child, and I told her Beryl was my mom.*

Your moms knew each other? Amari asked. *That's wild.*

Yes, Holly said. *It's really wild. Our moms were pregnant together! When my mom told us that, I was like, 'Wait! What?! You and who and what?!?!'*

I laughed. *But your mom just ignored you,* I said. *Kira came around the chair and crouched in front of me. Her face was all worried and sad. But it was happy too, remember?*

Holly nodded.

She brushed my hair back away from my forehead and said, 'Your mom and I used to go to Tom's diner over on Washington after our Lamaze classes. We'd order so much food, the waitress would always ask if someone was joining us.'

And then Kira laughed. And I remember I wanted to laugh too, but my heart felt like it was competing with my tongue for space inside my mouth. So I just whispered to Kira, 'You knew my mother.'

I stopped talking. It was hard to tell the story. But it wasn't hard. It felt like everyone in the room was leaning in and listening and really caring. Felt like everyone around me wanted everything to turn out all right.

We got you, Red, Amari said quietly. *You know that, right?*

I nodded, smiled at him and continued.

Kira told me how much I looked like my mother and how when she first saw me she thought maybe it was possible, but it was too much of a coincidence. But Brooklyn's small when you think about it, right?

Everyone nodded.

It must have been like . . . like a resurrection, Ashton said. *Like here was somebody that could answer your questions?*

Yes! I said. *That's so true! I had a million questions. There were, like, a million conversations I'd had in my mind with my mother. But the first thing I asked Holly's mom was what stuff my mom loved.*

I remember she looked really sad then, I said. *It was like she was going back to being with my mom and remembering everything about it. She thought for a long time, then finally said, 'Your mom loved to laugh. Even when things felt like they were falling apart, she found a way to laugh.'*

I wanted to ask what made my mom laugh. But I didn't. For some reason, knowing that she loved laughing was enough for that moment.

What about your dad, Esteban asked. *Did Kira know your dad too?*

I shook my head. *She never met him. Kira said once she and my mom became friends, they had, like, their ladies' thing going on.*

Like my mom with her girls, Amari said. *Eating all that food after going to spin class. Women are crazy.*

Both me and Holly said *Hey!* at the same time.

Amari threw his hands up. *You know I'm just messing with y'all.*

Tell them about the sun, Holly said. *The magic.*

Oh yeah! There's a high window in Holly's kitchen, I said. *And this crazy thing happened. The sky—like, it shifted, and everything got bright. And Kira laughed and said that she and my mom used to always talk about the light. How they thought light shifting was the dead sending us messages. Love messages. She said that every time the sun goes behind a cloud and then comes out again, that's a message from the other side.*

I looked over at Esteban. He was staring up at the sky as though he was waiting for the sun to send him a message. He had one hand in his pocket, and I knew he was touching his poem.

For the whole time that Kira was braiding my hair, I said, *she talked about my mother—what she remembered, how they lost touch, how she heard about the accident. And I told her all about my uncle and how he made me laugh and how he always told me that my laugh reminded him of my mom.*

I stopped talking. No one said anything for a long time. Holly smiled at me and nodded, giving me a thumbs-up. I felt lighter. Free somehow. Like I'd been carrying the weight of that story in me, not even knowing it was heavy. Like so many bricks had been lifted off me.

Esteban was hugging his legs again, but he was watching me now.

Your story makes me think that I'm happy my papi's alive, Haley. I mean, because of your story, I can feel . . . some hope, because no matter what, we're going to see him again. He didn't die and that's good. Even if everything has to change to be with him again? At least I could be with him again, right?

We all nodded.

He's still writing poetry, Esteban said. *And breathing.*

He looked at me. *Even though it's kinda sad, what happened and everything, it feels happy too, that we have each other. Like that thing Ms. Laverne said about how we have to harbor each other, you remember?*

I nodded.

I feel like your story does that. You're my same age and you have to be strong for your dad. It makes me feel like I can be strong too.

And everyone else said, *Yeah.*

Me too.

For real.

35

I turned off the recorder and put it back into my knapsack. It was almost three o'clock, but just like most Fridays now, none of us moved. We'd started ignoring the time weeks ago. It was strange to remember that we'd come into this room confused about why we were here. Now we could barely remember a time when we weren't here.

Hey! Amari said. *Since we all doing some sharing, before we all bounce for the weekend, I want to show you something.* He opened his drawing pad and we all leaned toward him. *I been copying some of these comic book guys,* Amari said. *I got some sweet characters. I'm gonna put all of y'all in there too. It's gonna be so, so tight. It's like my brain is frying with ideas.*

Amari had the biggest smile on his face that I'd ever

seen, which made the rest of us smile and look through the comics. Even me and Holly went over to see what the four of them were getting all excited about.

Some people try to hate on comics, but they get you inspired, you know, Amari said. *It's like—man! Like, look at this guy.*

He opened a Black Panther comic, and the Black Panther was big and black and strong on the page. Outside the ARTT room window, the school yard was bright and cold. The strange thing is, I don't remember any other sound but Amari's voice. There must have been kids playing. There must have been yelling and laughter and horns blowing, but none of it comes back to me. Just Amari's smile, his comic books, us gathering around him.

Like, what if the Black Panther was just a kid in this school, he said. *Just a regular kid. That's what I was thinking last night. Every comic book hero used to be a little kid in school once, so what if kids like us are the superheroes, right? The real superheroes.*

Amari was talking fast. The other boys were nodding as he turned the pages of the comic books.

Like Esteban, Amari said. *Who's the Dominican Superman? I mean, we got Miles Morales—he's the Puerto Rican Spider-Man, so we got Tiago covered. But Ashton—who's the superhero whose dad works at Key Food? And, like, for me—who's the guy who doesn't get to play with guns, so he has to find out another way to De-Stroy!*

Amari looked at me. *Haley—I got you too. Superhero Girl who lives with her uncle.*

I got you too, Holly. Your richness is your superpower.

I waited for Holly to get mad at Amari for calling her rich. But she didn't. She was even smiling a little. *I'll take it,* she said. *Just hook me up with a nice cape.*

We must have headed out soon after that, because I remember us all walking down the hall and out into the school yard together. We walked slowly, still talking.

36

What do you think your superpower would be? Holly asked me as we waited for Kira to pick us up after school. Someone had drawn a hopscotch game just outside the school yard fence and she started jumping up the numbers, then turning and jumping back down them again.

I had just been wondering that myself—wondering who the superhero is with a dad in prison.

I don't know, I said. *What about you?*

I'd want super focus. Super be-still-ness. I'd want to sit like a statue for hours and hours and be like a sponge. Everything anyone said to me would get soaked right up, and I'd be the most brilliant person ever.

But you're so smart already, Holly. Even if you can't sit still.

But imagine if I could. Then I'd be even smarter! I'd probably be graduating high school at, like, thirteen.

But then you wouldn't be in school with me, I said.

Oh yeah, that's right. Then I think I'd want us to have the same superpower.

Maybe I'd want to fly, I said.

Me too, she said. *That's easy. Everybody wants to fly. But what else?*

I thought about my dad. There was a room in my brain where I was mad at him. Some days I opened that door and it made me so sad that I just sat for hours staring off at nothing. Those were the days Ms. Laverne and my uncle and even Holly left me alone. Those were the days filled with gray light and cold, damp air. That was the room where I realized I couldn't forgive him.

I think, I said slowly. *I think I'd want to forget.*

Holly stopped jumping.

Forget what?

You know—about what happened between my mom and dad. I'd want to just imagine that I always had a dad. That I never had a mom.

But you did have a mom.

I know.

You'd want to forget even the little tiny bit you know about her? Holly frowned, confused.

It's not that. It's just I don't want to be sad and mad when I think about it all. I just want to think about the good stuff.

Then you want forgiveness, not forgetness, Holly said.

Forgiveness, I thought. I want forgiveness. Standing there, I realized I'd first have to forgive my father. Not forget. But forgive.

Holly started hopscotching again just as Kira pulled up in the car.

37

Check this out, Amari said to us on Monday morning. We were in the school yard before class, and the day was surprisingly warm. Amari opened his book and slowly started turning the pages. We all leaned in over the pictures. And there we were! On every single page. Tiago shooting webs from his hands over buildings and vans and cars, Esteban flying over an ocean and, far down below him, the same tiny man over and over again with a T-shirt on that said PAPI. Holly was Catwoman in a fancy building, her sneakers almost bigger than the rest of her, and we all laughed. When Amari turned the page again, there I was—my hair a mass of curly red wires that seemed to be shooting electricity.

That's tight, Ashton said.

It's like I've always had my superpower with me, I said. *I was born with red hair.*

Yup. Amari looked up at me and smiled. *That's the cool thing. There's all kinds of ways to get your superpower. You take somebody like Superman, who was born with his superpower, and somebody like Spider-Man—the way he got his power was kinda tragic, right? But then it became this good thing. That's what's up.*

That night, as I waited for my uncle to come say good night, I thought about Amari's drawing of me, about the brilliance of my hair, the superpower in it. And I thought about my mother and father. Tragedy is strange. It takes away. And it gives too. I couldn't ever imagine a life without my uncle, his laughing, his stories, the way he looks at the world. But until I saw Amari's drawing, I hadn't really thought about my hair. The power is both my mom and dad running through it, through me. And their moms and dads. And theirs. The *a* and *b* of me. The *c* and *d*, as Holly said. I smiled. My mother was gone, but she was continuing too. Inside of me. And that was its own superpower.

You ready? my uncle said. He stood in the doorway,

holding his guitar. Before my father went to prison, they played music together, my father on the piano, my uncle on the guitar. Lame songs about mountains and clouds and rainbows, my uncle said. But then when my father went away, my uncle started writing his own music, telling stories in his songs. Sometimes he played them for me. I liked falling asleep to the quiet hum of his guitar and his soft voice, the notes trembling.

My uncle had lived through it all, the car accident, my father being taken away, him suddenly being not just my uncle but my mom and dad too. He was my superhero.

Yeah, I said. I wanted to tell him about the day, but instead, I pulled the covers up over me and smiled. My uncle sat in the small chair at the foot of my bed and started strumming his guitar.

38

When we came back to school after Easter break, Esteban was gone.

Where? we asked Ms. Laverne.

Home to the Dominican Republic. The family left on Sunday.

But he didn't tell us, we said.

He didn't know, Ms. Laverne said. She said, *I'm sorry.* She said, *Let's just do what we want today.* She said, *I know you all will miss him terribly.* Amari looked at his drawings. Tiago put his head down on his desk. After a while, I could hear quiet sobbing. Ashton stared out the window. The sun was so bright, the buildings seemed sharp enough to cut someone. Holly got up and walked around the classroom, pulling books off the shelves and then putting them back again. After a few minutes, she went back to her seat, took out her knitting, then put it back. Then took it out again and started knitting, the needles clicking and scraping against each other.

I took out the recorder, turned the volume down low and played the last poem Esteban had read to us, his sweet voice filling the classroom.

And when his missing feels like it's going to
break him into pieces, tell him it won't.
Tell him that he is made of the iron
of grandfathers and grandmothers and
their grandfathers and grandmothers, people
who were human and worked hard and had dreams.
Tell him to hold on to his dreams because his abuela
and abuelo still believe in the power of dreams.
Tell him he is their dream.
And he is my dream.
And he is the dream come true
of the ancestors.
We are all the dream come true of the people
who came before us.
And when he asks, tell him I am fine.
Tell him I am free.
Tell him the mountains go on and on

and where they stop, Pico Duarte's peak points up
like lips
telling God a story. Maybe this mountain sings
of promises and families broken. Maybe
it holds inside it a beautifully remembered dream.
Tell him to hold inside himself
all good memories—hugs. Friends. Laughter.
Tomorrow holds no promises but now is not the time
for tears.

39

In June, just before the school year ended, we met in the ARTT room one last time.

Amari said, *I'm gonna miss you guys.*

Me too, Tiago said.

Me too, Ashton said. *You guys are awesome.*

There was air in the room where Esteban's *Me too* would have been. We had left his desk where it was, left the pillow he sat on in the window, and it felt like a ghost in the room, like he was still with us, telling us about his papi, baseball season, poetry.

Me too, I said, looking at his empty seat. I hoped he was in the Dominican Republic. I hoped that he and his papi were catching baseballs and swimming in the ocean. I hoped that the family was together and safe and happy.

Holly looked around at us. *It's just the summer, people. We'll be back together in September. It's not like it's for forever.*

True, Ashton said. *But it won't be like this. We won't be with you and Haley. It won't be the ARTT room.*

Yeah, Amari said. *But don't forget our promise. Every day gets us closer to twenty years from now, right?*

Yup, Holly said. *When we all meet back here, all old and gray and wobbly.*

I'm not gonna be old and wobbly, Amari said. *Maybe you will be, but not me.*

You already are *old and wobbly,* Holly said.

We laughed—even Amari.

Remember how scared we were the first time Ms. Laverne brought us in here? Holly said.

Yeah, I hated this room, Amari said. *It was, like, depressing. That one sad picture hanging on the closet.*

We looked at the kid's picture of the sun. It was as familiar as time now, something we saw but didn't see. It was beautiful.

And a lot of us didn't know each other, Tiago said. *We all just were like, 'What's this thing?'*

And it was us, I said. *That thing that we were so scared of was just us together.*

Yup, Tiago said. He smiled at me, his glasses glinting.

Beneath them, I noticed how pretty his eyes were. *Isn't that crazy?*

And Esteban, Ashton said softly. *Esteban was here. Never gonna forget Esteban.*

We all got quiet.

Some part of him is still here, Holly said.

Yeah, Amari said. *That's true.*

Yeah, the rest of us said.

We still have his voice and his dad's poetry, I said. *He left that for us. For us to keep forever.*

Amari opened his drawing pad and flipped through the pages until he came to a brightly colored picture.

That's us, he said. *And that's a harbor.* He carefully tore the drawing from his book. Then, without saying anything, he walked over to the picture of the sun, pulled one of the thumbtacks from it and hung his picture beside it.

We all stared at it. It was us. And like the picture of the sun, it too was beautiful.

40

The light has shifted now and the Ailanthus tree has turned to a shadow in the dusk. I turn the recorder off and sit on my bed. I can hear the soft swish of the ceiling fan in the hallway. Outside, little kids on the block are playing a game of tag, yelling, *Not it! Not it!* Then a woman's voice breaks through, calling someone home to dinner.

I uncurl my legs from beneath me and head for the stairs. But at the top of the stairs I stop and sit, watching my father at the piano as he lifts his fingers from the keys and presses them down again. His fingers are long and white and delicate. I'd never really looked at his hands. But as they move over the piano keys, lifting such sweet music out of them, I want to run down and hug him. I want to tell him about my year in the ARTT room, about everything he missed in the many years he was in prison.

I want to ask him if he had great friends when he was my age. Friends he promised to meet up with again in twenty years.

But I stare at his back as he plays. He is somewhere else. He is with my mother in another dream. A dream of a place before this place. A time before this time. A story before this story.

Soon my uncle will be finished packing and will come down to join him on his guitar. Maybe they'll ask me to sing and my voice will be high and off-key and they'll laugh about how the musical gene skipped right over me.

When I was in fifth grade, I didn't know how fast time could move. How you could wake up one day and so much around you had changed forever. I didn't know that one day we'd have a teacher who would say, *Take your books. You won't be coming back here today.* And that we'd walk out of the lives we'd always known, our faces turned toward her, so many questions and so much fear.

Daddy, I say. My father turns from the piano and looks up at me.

Play 'Summertime.'

My father looks confused for a minute, and then his face softens into something warm and familiar. Something I knew a lifetime ago when I was a tiny girl getting tossed into the air by him, laughing and screaming, both afraid and thrilled.

When I was in fifth grade, I didn't know the Unfamiliar would be beautiful and funny and heartbreaking and hard. That it would be Amari calling me Red and the glint coming off of Tiago's glasses. That it would be Esteban in the window, a silhouette with the sun coming in around him. That it would be poems and pictures and questions. And answers.

I head down the stairs and sit on the bench beside my father. His fingers are long and pale and stretched out across the keys. He smiles, bends and kisses the top of my head, the first notes of "Summertime" rising from the piano.

I dreamed this moment a thousand times, he says.

I didn't know it would be people you barely knew becoming friends that harbored you. And dreams you didn't even know you had—coming true. I didn't know it would be superpowers rising up out of tragedies, and perfect moments in a nearly empty classroom.

Me too, I say. And when I rest my head against his arm, when the music circles around us, when my uncle stops packing and joins in with his guitar and we pick up the song as if we'd always been singing it, what I know for sure now is that this is the end of one of many stories.

And also a beginning.

ACKNOWLEDGMENTS

Grateful to all the people who helped me write during such a crazy time in our country. You all know who you are, so I'm going to skip the names here. What I will say is harbor each other. Even strangers. Every day.

Jacqueline Woodson

PRAISE FOR JACQUELINE WOODSON

"Ms. Woodson writes with a sure understanding of the thoughts of young people, offering a poetic, eloquent narrative that is not simply a story . . . but a mature exploration of grown-up issues and self-discovery."

—The New York Times Book Review

BROWN GIRL DREAMING

National Book Award winner • NAACP Image Award winner • Coretta Scott King Award winner • Newbery Honor winner • Sibert Honor winner • *New York Times* bestseller

"This is a book full of poems that cry out to be learned by heart."***—The New York Times Book Review***

"Gorgeous."***—Vanity Fair***

"Moving and resonant . . . captivating."***—Wall Street Journal***

"A radiantly warm memoir."***—Washington Post***

★ "An extraordinary—indeed brilliant—portrait of a writer as a young girl."***—The Horn Book,*** **starred review**

★ "Vivid."***—The Bulletin of the Center for Children's Books,*** **starred review**

★ "Mesmerizing."***—School Library Journal,*** **starred review**

★ "A marvel."—***Booklist,*** **starred review**

★ "Will linger long after the page is turned."—***Kirkus Reviews,*** **starred review**

★ "Clear, evocative language. . . . A beautifully crafted work."
—***Library Media Connection,*** **starred review**

★ "Sharp images and poignant observations seen through the eyes of a child."—***Publishers Weekly,*** **starred review**

FEATHERS

Newbery Honor winner

★ "With her usual talent for creating characters who confront, reflect, and grow into their own persons . . . the story ends with hope and thoughtfulness while speaking to those adolescents who struggle with race, faith, and prejudice."—***School Library Journal,*** **starred review**

★ "The heroine is able to see beyond it all—to look forward to a time when the pain subsides and life continues."
—***Publishers Weekly,*** **starred review**

AFTER TUPAC AND D FOSTER

Newbery Honor winner

★ "A memorable, affecting novel about the sustaining power of love and friendship."—***Booklist,*** **starred review**

★ "The emotions and high-quality writing make it a book well worth recommending."—***School Library Journal,*** **starred review**

★ "The subtlety and depth with which the author conveys the girls' relationships lend this novel exceptional vividness and staying power."—***Publishers Weekly,*** **starred review**

MIRACLE'S BOYS

Coretta Scott King Award winner • *Los Angeles Times* Book Prize winner

★ "Readers will be caught up in this searing and gritty story. . . . Woodson composes a plot without easy answers."
***—Kirkus Reviews,* starred review**

HUSH

National Book Award finalist

"Complex coming-of-age story. . . . Images and characters who are impossible to forget."***—School Library Journal***

"Readers facing their own identity crises will find familiar conflicts magnified and exponentially compounded here, yet instantly recognizable and optimistically addressed."
—Publishers Weekly

"Intellectually engaging . . . will give youngsters plenty to think about."***—Kirkus Reviews***

LOCOMOTION

National Book Award finalist • Coretta Scott King Honor winner

★ "Moving, lyrical, and completely convincing."***—Kirkus Reviews*, starred review**

★ "A masterful use of voice."***—School Library Journal*, starred review**

★ "Skillfully and artfully composed."***—The Horn Book*, starred review**

PEACE, LOCOMOTION

★ "Moving, thought-provoking, and brilliantly executed, this is the rare sequel that lives up to the promise of its predecessor."—***School Library Journal*, starred review**

"Characters that readers will feel close to."—***Kirkus Reviews***

"Moving . . . Spare, beautiful prose . . . lyrical. . . . The simple words are packed with longing and are eloquent about the 'little things people don't think real hard about,' little things that reveal the big issues of family, community, displacement, war, and peace."—***Booklist***

"Woodson creates a full-bodied character in kind, sensitive Lonnie. Readers will understand his quest for peace, and appreciate the hard work he does to find it."—***Publishers Weekly***

IF YOU COME SOFTLY

ALA Best Book for Young Adults

★ "Once again, Woodson handles delicate, even explosive subject matter with exceptional clarity, surety and depth."

—***Publishers Weekly*, starred review**